BOUND
FOR HOME

BOUND FOR HOME

MEIKA HASHIMOTO

SCHOLASTIC INC.

Copyright © 2022 by Meika Hashimoto

This book was originally published in hardcover by Scholastic Press in 2022.

ISBN 978-1-338-57223-0

10 9 8 7 6 5 4   22 23 24 25 26

Printed in the U.S.A.   40

This edition first printing January 2022

Book design by Stephanie Yang

For Emile, Buckey, Piper, and Marzipan.
When I'm with you, I'm home.

CHAPTER 1

EMI

THE SWEAT TRICKLED down from Emi's scalp, weaving its way through her hair until it slid, itchy and warm, across the nape of her neck. She sat, trying to keep still as a stone, her back pressed against the rough bark of an oak tree, listening to the snorts of the bear behind her.

It was ripping through a honeycomb, gobbling up the hunks of honey-dipped wax, unbothered by the enraged bees trying to penetrate its rough fur with their tiny venom-tipped stingers.

Emi glanced down at the dog wriggling in her arms. His panting mouth was lifted in a sloppy, pink, dippy smile, but there was a determined wiggle to his butt that meant business. For some reason she could not understand, Max was fighting her.

"Shh, Max, shh. We have to be quiet," she whispered to him.

Behind her, the bear grunted. The bushes rustled, twigs snapping under its weight. She could hear it panting.

Emi's muscles tensed, screaming at her to flee. But she knew Max would never be able to keep up with her. Not with only three good legs. She had to keep him hidden. She had to keep him safe.

Max had other ideas. With a powerful squirm, he pulled out of her arms and lunged around the tree, a whine in his throat.

Emi sprang up to bring him back and found Max standing motionless, paw raised and nose pointed, his eyes glued to something that the bear was heading toward. She followed his gaze past the bear to a bright patch of silky red fur shining through the grass in the middle of the field.

It was a cat. And for some reason, Emi's goofball of a dog was willing to risk exposure to a four-hundred-pound predator in order to protect it.

Emi's heart skipped a beat. A pulse of fear rose up through her throat. Even when she swallowed, she could still taste it. As she watched the cat leap away toward the opposite end of the field with the bear closing in on it, Max began to howl.

"Max, what are you doing?" Emi cried, expecting the bear to train its ravenous eyes on them.

Max howled again, and the cat turned. Although Emi was running for her life, she looked back, and in that moment, Emi saw that the cat knew Max. And that Max knew the cat and cared for it. And somehow, in knowing that, Emi understood the cat was something that she had to protect, too. Because Max, with his injured leg, couldn't.

Max took a step forward.

Emi tapped his snout once, gently. "Sit," she whispered. She would not let Max put himself in danger. Not again. She leaned close to Max and brought her face up to his. Her dark chestnut eyes met his big chocolate ones.

Max took another step.

"Sit," Emi repeated.

Max stood; his head tilted to one side. Emi could almost see the wheels whirling around in his brain. He didn't sit, but he also didn't move.

Emi kissed him on his nose, once. Then she straightened herself up and strode around the tree to face a hungry bear over a cat.

As she charged, she heard a rustle behind her.

No. No, no, no.

Max was coming. And there was no time to do anything about it.

CHAPTER 2
MAX

Max's Guide to Escaping from
the Local Animal Shelter: Attempt #7

1. The night before attempt #7, use your teeth. Chew. Chew. Chew. Eventually, you'll get through those pesky metal bars.

2. Then, in the morning, wait until after kibble time. Breakfast is the best six seconds of the day and should not be abandoned for ANY reason.

3. Do not attempt an escape while humans are in the

room. Especially if they have collars or nets. Or are very fast. Or know you've tried to escape six times and watch your every tail wag.

4. Once you've gnawed your way out of the kennel, you still have to make it down the hallway, past all the other barking dogs (don't stop to sniff butts or you'll lose precious time), and beyond the receptionist's desk.

5. You haven't made it past that desk yet, but you're confident that once you do, an exit door can't be far away. The humans have got to leave from *somewhere*.

6. If you make it outside, you're free. There's no reason why the shelter staff would chase you down. Absolutely no reason at all.

When the kennel room door opened and the lights clicked on, signaling the start of a new day, Max stopped chewing the bars of his cage and studied his work. In the dark, he could have sworn that the bars were about to give way. Now, looking at them, he could see that the clever humans had won that round. The bars were covered with his spit, and there were flattened little dents in the metal, but the bars were still very much intact.

Attempt #7 was no good.

It was time for attempt #8! Max stood in his kennel, his tail thumping, as he watched a shelter worker drag a rolling bin full of dog food across the floor. When she reached the first kennel, she opened the bin and withdrew a scoop half-full of kibble. Opening the kennel door, she dropped the kibble into the dog's food bowl. Max could hear the snuffing and snorting of the dog gobbling up his food.

The woman opened four more kennel doors before she reached Max.

"Good morning, Max," she said, opening his door and dumping a scoop of kibble into his bowl. "Chow time!"

Max woofed. The food never changed, but he loved every bite. After devouring each little piece of kibble, he licked his bowl, around his bowl, and under his bowl, then his chops to make sure he had gotten every last bit.

Breakfast had been eaten. It was time for *ESCAPE*!

A few minutes later, another staff member came into the room. She clipped a leash to Max's collar. "Play time, buddy!" she told him. She gathered four more dogs from their cages. Leading the dogs out of the kennel room, she marched everyone down the hallway and toward a door that led to the outdoor play area.

As they reached the door, Max impulsively made his move. He leaped over one of the other dogs, then threaded his body under another, tangling his leash between the two of them. Then he grabbed his leash in his mouth and tugged as hard as he could. All the dogs collided together into a mess of yelps and teeth.

The shelter worker lost her hold on all the leashes as the dogs descended into furry chaos.

Max ducked under the other dogs and bolted toward the front of the animal shelter. Skidding around a corner, nails scrabbling along the waxed floor, he slipped and did a full rollover, his giant paws tumbling in the air, before regaining his footing. As he galloped past the receptionist's desk, his heart thumped happily. He'd done it! He had gone farther than he'd ever gone before!

Something hard hit him square in the snout, and he bounced back, confused. He shook his head, ears flapping against his cheeks, then ran forward again. Just before his nose collided for a second time with the invisible wall, he caught a glimpse of a dog staring at him. Big wide eyes.

Short brown fur. A blunt head that seemed too big for its body, and one long tongue dangling from its mouth.

Hey, that looks like my *tongue,* Max thought as he hit the glass door, leaving a trail of slobber in his wake.

"Gotcha!" The shelter worker grabbed Max's collar and quickly clipped a leash to it. "You're going straight back where you came from," she scolded as she led him to his kennel, then locked the door.

Max peered out from between the bars and thumped his tail.

Tomorrow. There was always tomorrow for escape attempt #9.

CHAPTER 3

EMI

THE PISCATAQUIS COUNTY animal shelter was a squat yellow building with a sloped tin roof, along which a line of icicles dropped down like a row of jagged teeth. It was only February, but three months of Maine winter storms had already left hulking snowbanks piled up along the sidewalk.

A rusty gray pickup truck pulled into the parking lot and came to a halt. From the passenger seat, Emi heard the engine click off. For a few moments, she sat stiffly, listening to the ticking of the metal as it cooled.

She peeled back the wrapper of her Snickers bar, the soothing crinkle of plastic in her ears as she exposed the lush dark brown chocolate underneath. She finished up the last bite and shoved the wrapper deep into her pocket. The candy-peanut-nougat taste swirled around her mouth, intoxicating. As she swallowed, comfort and relief flowed down her throat.

Emi knew that the pinpoint of sugary joy would soon be replaced by a crash that would send her stomach and feelings plummeting. But food was a comfort for her ever since her mom had died. A bag of Cheetos or a toasted strawberry Pop-Tart could distract her senses and take her mind off her problems.

"Well, now," said Jim as he pulled the key from the ignition. "We're here." He dropped the key into the pocket of his faded winter coat and patted the salt-and-pepper hair poking out from his thick winter cap. "You ready to meet some dogs?" he asked.

Emi avoided her foster dad's eyes. "You know, I really don't have to be part of this. I'll probably be gone in a few weeks anyway, and whatever dog we pick won't even have the chance to get to know me." She hated how the words sounded—whiny and ungrateful—but she threw them out anyway. They were her protection.

Protection. Emi's hand automatically touched a slim jade bracelet around her wrist. She twisted it, like she always did when she thought about that word.

The bracelet had been given to her three years ago, on her

ninth birthday. "It will keep you safe," her mom had told her, sliding the ring of green-and-white stone past Emi's hand and onto her left wrist, where it hung tight as an embrace. Emi had promised her mom she would never take it off.

Then her mom had died a year later, and with her father gone, lost in a lobster boating accident right before she had been born, Emi had become completely alone. The bracelet had been the only thing that she had been allowed to take with her.

That was when she had started using her words as a shield to keep herself from needing to trust or depend on anyone else. After three foster placements in three different towns, Emi was tired of trying to get close to people. Of smiling and acting grateful and cloaking her rage and hurt at being shuffled around like a deck of cards behind *thank yous* and *yes pleases*.

And when her newest foster family, Jim and Meili (she couldn't and wouldn't call them Dad and Mom even though they had suggested it a month ago, on the first day she had come into their house, which had been so tidy and cozy it had made her want to suffocate), had asked if she would be okay if they adopted a dog, Emi had said, "Sure, whatever," without actually meaning it.

"Meili and I have been looking to get a dog for some time, and we want you to help us choose," Jim said. "And I don't think you'll be gone so fast. We like you, Emi. And even though you don't want to believe it, we want you with us."

"Fine." Emi fumbled for her seat belt and unclicked it. She crammed a chunky woolen hat onto her head before stepping out into the frosty morning.

Picking her way across the black ice, she waddled her feet like a penguin, with her arms stretched out, until she reached the safety of the sidewalk. Her boots found traction as they crunched against the road salt, and she was able to walk steadily up to the glass double doors that served as an entrance.

Just as she reached it, she saw a dog pelting past the front desk, a long leash snaking behind him. Before she could react, he leaped up and plastered himself straight into the glass, his nose squashed not an inch away from her stomach.

Emi stood frozen as the dog looked up at her, his dark brown eyes full of astonished surprise. He backed up and shook his head, then ran at the door again. Before he could reach it, a woman ran up to him and grasped his collar.

"Not again, Max!" The woman's voice was muffled from behind the door, but Emi heard the dog's name clear as a bell.

As the woman led Max back past the front desk, Emi pulled open the door and went inside.

"Hello, dear." A silver-haired woman with tortoiseshell glasses perched upon her nose glanced at Emi from behind the desk. "May I help you?"

"Yes. My foster father is looking to adopt a dog," Emi said, her voice loud and firm.

"That's right, Barbara," said Jim from behind her. He took off his jacket and folded it under his arm. "We were wondering if you had any that were good for a kid Emi's age."

"Jim!" The woman beamed. "Good to see you. It's been a while."

Jim nodded. "Last time I saw you, you were just about to get hip surgery."

Barbara patted her side. "Got it replaced with titanium and plastic, and it's as good as new. I'm even back to Tuesday-night hockey again."

"Barbara is the best goalie this side of the river," Jim explained to Emi.

Emi rolled her eyes. "Can we just get to the dogs?" she asked.

She expected Barbara to be taken aback at her abruptness, but the older woman just laughed.

"Girl has no time for chitchat," Barbara said. "I can understand that. When I was her age, I found old-people talk boring, too." She stood up. "I'll go get Tess—she'll introduce you to the animals." She went into the hallway behind the desk.

A few moments later, Tess appeared. She was the same woman Emi had seen catching the runaway mutt.

"I hear you want to look at some dogs," Tess said, giving Emi a quick glance before turning to Jim. "What kind are you looking for?" she asked him.

Jim coughed. "Well, I think Emi should be in charge of that question," he said.

Emi lifted her gaze and spoke as clearly as she could. "What dog has been here the longest?" She wanted a dog that nobody else would take. Even though she had no doubt that she would be gone soon, off to yet another foster home once she messed up so badly that Jim and Meili wouldn't want her anymore, at least the dog would find a home with them.

Tess raised her eyebrows, but instead of acting shocked, like Emi expected, she laughed. "I've been waiting for someone like you," she told Emi, her face relaxing into a smile. She motioned for Emi and Jim to follow her down a hallway that smelled of wet fur and disinfectant, and stopped in front of a big blue door.

"Come on inside," she said.

Beyond the door was a large room filled with cages. As Emi walked among them, *Snow White and the Seven Dwarfs* came to her mind.

She saw a Labrador retriever puppy with big brown eyes madly chasing its long, furry tail. Way too adorable. Emi thought about the seven dwarfs again. *That Lab would be Happy. He'll have no trouble finding a home.*

A snoring basset hound with ears folded over its head was Sleepy. He looked like the most boring dog in the world.

Bashful was in the corner, a quivering dachshund trying to turn its hot-dog body into a tight bagel in the far corner of its kennel. Nope.

Grumpy was a slobbery bulldog drinking sulkily from a bowl of water. Emi stopped in front of Grumpy. She kind of liked his big, lumpy face, but then Tess called her over, and that's when she saw Dopey.

His oversize head was pressed up against the front of his cage, his jaws happily gnawing away at the thick metal bars. Short, sand-colored fur barely hid his pale pink skin, which was completely exposed along his underbelly. When

Emi approached him, his ears perked up and he woofed at her, a bit of drool falling from his mouth.

"Huh," Emi said. She poked a finger through the cage, trying to scratch his head.

"Emi, no touching until we know what that dog's like," Jim's voice warned her.

"This is . . . ," Tess began.

"Max," Emi finished. "I saw him at the front entrance." She turned to Tess. "He's been here the longest?"

Tess hesitated before answering. "He has. And he's actually very friendly. But . . . he's a pit bull mix."

Emi waited for Tess to continue, but she didn't. When the silence went on for too long, Emi asked, "So?"

"A pit bull can have a reputation for being vicious," Tess explained. "But that's just because they're often used in illegal dogfighting, where the dogs are trained to be extremely aggressive and to attack other dogs. When raised in a loving household, pit bulls can be the sweetest dogs around."

Emi looked down at Max. He had stopped gnawing at the bars and peered at her, his head cocked to one side. He looked even dumber than Grumpy.

"Max is hard to place because a lot of people can't see past what they think he'll be," Tess continued. "He was surrendered to the shelter by a family when they had their first child. Max hadn't done anything, but the family was worried that he could bite the baby at any moment, and they didn't want to take that risk." She reached between the bars and patted Max on the head. "Most dogs only last a month or two at the shelter. Max has been here for nine, and at this rate, he's going to be a shelter dog for life."

Emi imagined herself in Max's place, watching hundreds of families pass by, never looking twice at this barrel-chested, yellow-toothed ball of muscle and fur that no one wanted to protect.

She gripped Max's cage between her fingers. Her jade bracelet clinked gently against the metal. She twisted the bracelet, once.

"I'll take him," she said.

CHAPTER 4
MAX

MAX THREW UP in the truck. He hadn't meant to; it was just that the shelter worker had given him a final bowl of kibble before his long, windy ride toward wherever he was going. He was in the front, panting from stress, sandwiched between the girl and the man, the girl holding on to his collar, when the whole bowl full of kibble got a running start out of his stomach and came exploding through his mouth.

His vomit landed everywhere—on the girl, on the man, on the seat of the truck, on the floor of the truck, on his paws. Another heave left a splatter of brown gunk on the windshield, and if Max had not felt so sick, he would have been impressed with himself.

"Gross! Stop! We've got to stop!" the girl cried.

"Emi, we're almost back at the house," the man replied. "Just hang on for two more miles."

"But . . ."

"We can't do anything right now. We've got no rags or paper towels in the truck—we have to wait until we can get some from home."

"Ugh, fine," said the girl.

The man shook his head and fell silent. Max noticed that there was some puke on the steering wheel. He leaned over and licked it up, then started cleaning his paws and the seat next to him.

"Thanks, boy. Wouldn't have wanted to put my hand in that." The man laughed.

"Ew. Ew, ew, ewwww," the girl said.

Max paid her no mind. Food was food. By the time he had finished re-eating all that was in reach, the truck had pulled into a short driveway, the tires crunching against the ice-slicked dirt. The man parked next to a small wooden house with a plume of smoke drifting from the brick chimney.

The girl opened the door, and Max hopped out. He sniffed the air, feeling the cold, crisp freedom of it. Here was his chance to escape!

He bolted toward the woods—and the leash stopped him mid-stride.

Oops. So much for attempt #9. As Max was pulled back, he caught a glimpse of amused eyes peering out at him from the shadows behind a stone wall.

He flipped around and raced toward the house, dragging the girl behind him, where a nice lady opened the door for him, and he hurtled inside.

The first thing he did was to put his nose down and sniff everything he could find. He smelled his way past a shoe bench, knocking over the boots that lay underneath it, around a soapstone woodstove pumping out waves of heat, onto a worn brown couch with cushions that smelled of lost popcorn and copper pennies, into the kitchen, where he licked up a smattering of cookie crumbs and tomato sauce before being shooed away by the nice lady, whose face had gone from smiling to alarmed just as he was about to bite down on a gob of peanut butter that appeared to be resting on some kind of wooden block with a metal hinge and a picture of holey cheese on its front, into a bathroom that provided nothing of interest, past a couple of closed doors, and back into the living room, where he promptly had a nice long pee on the carpet.

He chose his spot carefully, sniffing around until he found the corner that smelled just right. No cobwebs, no dust, and just a whiff of feline scent that he decided to cover right up.

After attempt #8, the shelter had forgotten to bring him outside before returning him to his kennel, so Max had a whole night's worth of liquid to unleash. He lifted his leg and let go, a smile of relief streaked across his face.

The girl saw him and began to yell. Startled, Max peed harder. The girl crossed the carpet over to him and scooped him up in her arms. She lugged him out to the front porch and down the steps, droplets flying everywhere, until they reached the driveway and Max was allowed to finish peeing in peace.

Once he was done, he made a beeline toward the main road, but a loud yell from the girl chasing him from behind made him change his mind. Instead, he swung around and galloped back toward the house, nimbly dodging the girl's outstretched arms. When he reached the edge of the plowed driveway, he scrabbled up the hardened, crusted-over snow-bank, leash flying behind him, and leaped toward the freedom of the woods behind the house.

Attempt #10 and he was finally *free*!

CHAPTER 5
RED

RED WAS JUST about to start her afternoon mouse hunt when the truck wheezed in front of the house and jerked to a stop. From her vantage point on top of the woodshed, she could see the humans inside it. It was the man and the girl. Something was sitting directly on the girl, pawing at the window while she struggled with the latch. When the girl opened the door, the thing exploded out of the truck, tongue hanging, paws flailing.

A dog, Red thought in disgust. *I don't understand what humans see in them. Don't they know that dogs are nothing but trouble? They dig up gardens and make messes inside the house and destroy slippers.* She licked her long fur and slipped through a hole in the shed, where she had made a little home for herself.

When the previous owners had left the area a year ago,

Red had been in the woods hunting. She had not seen the moving truck lurch into the driveway or her family load all their possessions into it. She did not hear the boy call her name, over and over. She had been off on her own adventure, pursuing squirrels and mice under the fresh-fallen leaves of autumn.

Then, when she had returned, her family was gone. The house had been locked and shuttered, the scent of the family already fading.

Despite herself, Red had felt disappointed. She had grown to respect the boy, even perhaps love him. He had been kind to her, leaving out tins of tuna and bowls of dry kibble in the winter when food was scarce, and never asking her to leave the shed that she called home to become his captive inside the house.

She would have abandoned the familiar woods to follow him, perhaps even allowed herself to become an indoor cat. But the boy was gone, Red was alone, and she would not make the mistake of trusting a human with her affection again.

After all, she did not need them. Like her hardy Maine coon ancestors, Red was built to survive harsh winters on her own. Her coat had grown long and silky, and her ears sprouted tufts of fur that kept them warm. Her double paws kept her afloat above the snow, and her large size gave even the boldest of coyotes pause.

When her family left her, rather than seek out new humans, Red had made her home in the shed and spent months surviving on the rodents that had scurried in expecting shelter from the winter. The only warmth they ended up finding was the inside of her belly.

Then the new family had arrived. It had been a man and a woman, with a pickup and a small moving truck full of furniture and boxes. Two months after that, the girl had come home with them.

Red had been wary of making herself known. She knew she could make it just fine without humans, and she wasn't sure how the new people would react to her. So she kept her presence to the shed, which they had never opened, and observed them from a distance when they went out.

This afternoon, Red was curious enough about the new arrival that she risked slipping out of the shed for a better look. She crept behind a stone wall and watched as the girl was dragged by the dog into the house. As they crossed the entrance, the dog lifted his furry head and looked around.

He stuck out a long pink tongue and caught a snowflake. Despite herself, Red felt a flicker of amusement.

What a dope, she thought.

The dog turned his head and peered across the driveway to where Red was hidden. His eyes met hers, and he whined.

Red settled into a crouch, slinking along the wall and behind a big oak tree to keep hidden. She watched as the humans and the dog went into the house.

A few minutes later, she heard the creak of the front door of the house opening. There was a small cry, and the scatter of feet across the snow. Red poked her head out from behind the oak trunk just as a streak of canine fur scrambled past her.

"Come back!" cried the girl. She stood in the doorway, pulling on her boots, losing vital seconds as the dog galloped into the forest.

Red watched the girl take off after the escaped dog. As he disappeared into the thick pines, the girl went after him.

Red hesitated, one paw lifted uncertainly while she debated whether to take a nap or to interfere. Her whiskers quivered in the closest thing to a sigh, and she stepped forward and into the snow.

She followed the dog and the girl into the frozen woods. It was quiet except for the sound of the girl's fast breathing and the shuffle of her boots against the snow.

Red kept apace of the girl, staying to her side and out of sight, a silent stalker in the woods. Red had no trouble keeping up. The girl floundered in the deep snow, obviously unused to it, but kept going with stubborn determination. She went on until she came to a frozen stream. The dog had jumped it easily, but when the girl stepped onto the black ice, a spiderweb of cracks appeared and her foot plummeted through the ice. She withdrew it with a cry and stepped back.

Then, as if all her determination had seeped out of her cold, soaked foot, the girl fell against the snowbank. Her head sank into her chest. Red could see water slipping down her cheeks.

After a long time, the girl cleared her throat and dashed a hand across her face. She pulled a small package from her coat and tore it open. Tilting her head back, she poured color-ful round pieces into her mouth and crunched down on them with bitter, practiced strength. When she was done, she crossed her arms and dug her fingers into her skin as if she were trying to keep her body from dissolving.

It was beginning to get colder. Red waited for the girl to show an instinct for self-preservation and head back to the warmth of the house. But as the afternoon light slid lower through the trees, still the girl did not rise. Instead, she stuck her hands deep into her pockets and stared with fixed eyes in the direction of the cracked ice.

It was the dog the girl was waiting for, Red realized.

She scoffed at how foolish they both were. Each making simple mistakes that they thought nothing of, but that Red knew could cost their lives. But as she sat there looking at the little girl, Red decided as she licked her paws languidly, that she would help.

She twisted her head and looked at the dog tracks on the other side of the stream. Then she leaped onto the frozen ice, balanced herself, and leaped again, clearing the stream.

Bounding through the powdered snow, Red hunted the runaway dog up the side of the mountain. She had no trouble following his pawprints as they hurtled through the brush, mindless of the easier paths that the wild animals had already navigated. When she reached the dog, he was staring up at the darkening sky, as if the setting of the sun and the coming of night was a new thing for him.

"Hey, dummy," Red said to the dog.

The dog's ears shot straight up, and a startled bark

escaped his throat. "Who—who—whooo are you?" he asked, shivering as he spoke.

"I'm Red."

"Hi—hi—hiiiii, Red, I'mmmmm Max," said Max, shivering.

Red walked around Max once, sniffing at him. "Nothing of you smells like the earth and forest. You have no idea what to do out here, do you?" She didn't wait for him to answer. "The woods is no place for a soft, tasty dog. I'm surprised the coyotes haven't found you yet."

"Coyotes?" Max's nose quivered.

"They're related to you. Only they're wild. And they eat everything." Red stared at Max. Her stern green eyes glittered. "Everything."

Max pawed at the snow. "But I'm free! You d-d-don't understand—this is the moment I've been waiting for! I'll just dig—dig—dig a hole and hide tonight. If I make it deep—deep enough, they won't find me."

"No." Red's tail lashed to the side. "You are going to follow me back to the girl, and the two of you are going to go home right now. Neither of you are old enough nor smart enough to make it out here alone."

"B-but . . . ," Max started.

Red held up a paw. "Do not make me swipe you." She extended six sharp claws from her double paw and watched Max's tail take a sudden droop.

"Let's go," snapped Red. She turned and began to retrace her steps back to the girl, her gait strong and sure. She could hear footsteps behind her, wobbly and clumsy, but they kept up as she led Max to the cracked and frozen stream where the girl sat waiting.

CHAPTER 6
MAX

Max's Guide to a Somewhat Awkward Reunion

1. When you see the girl, bark happily through your chattering teeth. Now the coyotes have two soft, yummy things to choose from instead of just you!

2. Cross the stream to say hello. Then, when the girl lifts her head and looks like she wants to both hug and murder you at the same time, pause.

3. Remember that you've worked so hard for attempt #10 to succeed.

4. Have second thoughts about going back toward the

girl because it looks like the murder instead of the hug in her eyes is winning.

5. Turn around.

6. See the cat.

7. Turn back around. The girl is less scary than the cat.

8. When the girl lunges at you, decide that maybe both are equally scary.

9. Dart left as the girl goes right.

10. Dart right as the girl goes left.

11. Dart left as the girl goes left.

12. Realize your mistake as you feel the girl's fingers under your collar.

13. Hear the word *gotcha* for the second time. Begin to understand what it means.

14. Wriggle. Wriggle. Wriggle some more.

15. The girl pulls you one way; you pull the other way. It's a tug-of-war—fun!

16. Realize you are losing as the girl pulls you, inch by inch, back through the woods, up the porch steps, and into the house.

While the girl stamped her boots on a rough mat next to the door, Max shook, snow flying off his back, as he dried off. He spotted a large metal bowl filled with water along the side of the living room wall and lapped at it thirstily.

And lapped.

And lapped.

When the water was gone, he burped, regurgitated some slimy saliva water in his mouth, swallowed it back down, and then walked over to the girl, who was staring at him with what looked like just a hint of awe.

"I can't believe you drank all that," she told him. "You camel."

Max burped again, then waddled over to a blanket that had been set by the woodstove. He turned around a few times and plopped down, nestling his nose into the blanket until his entire face was mostly covered except for his eyes.

Hiding his muzzle, Max began to nibble on the blanket as he watched the girl spray some kind of liquid onto the carpet spots where he had peed. She had a roll of paper towels and mopped up the mess, starting from the living room corner all the way to the front door. When she was done, Max had successfully gnawed a dinner-plate-size hole in the blanket.

Much later in the evening, the girl called to Max and scooped some kibble into a bowl next to the refilled water bowl. Max hurried over to his dinner and wolfed it down. He began another long slurping journey with his water, emptying the bowl once more.

Right before bed, the girl took him outside. She stood in the gleam of the porch light as Max whizzed in the snow by the steps, his leash secured in both hands, wrapped three times across her palms.

Max gave a half-hearted tug toward the woods, but he wasn't really feeling like it was an appropriate time for attempt #11. It was too cold and too dark to do anything other than retreat back inside, where the girl opened one of the doors that had been closed earlier that day and led him into a plain, white-painted room with a wooden desk, a chair, and a small bed.

In the corner next to the bed was a cage.

He ran for the door, but it was already shut. The girl gathered him up in her arms and unloaded him into the cage before pulling the door shut, locking him inside.

The cage was far more deluxe than the one that Max had had at the shelter. There was a thick cotton dog bed inside it, and on top of the bed was a stuffed dinosaur toy that made his mouth water.

He should have felt lucky, but when the girl got into her bed and turned off the lamp on her nightstand, a helpless whine skittered out of his throat. He tried to drown it by gnawing at the dino plush, but when the T. rex's head had been chewed right off, he still felt the ugly knot of panic rise in his chest.

It wasn't long ago when he had gotten himself trapped inside a dumpster. He had been hunting for scraps outside a bakery. Following his nose, he had jumped inside it to feast on old bread and doughnuts but had made the mistake of stuffing himself into a stupor and settling down for a nap.

He had awoken to the thud of a trash bag beside him and the window of light from the open dumpster blinking out as the lid slid shut over it.

Eh, I have plenty of food, I'll be okay, Max had thought, and had continued with his nap. Hours later, he finally woke up and stretched, ready to be let out. But when he barked, no one came.

He had remained in the dumpster for two days, barking and whining as the smell of rotting butter and rancid bread grew stronger. He didn't mind eating spoiled food, but there was nothing to drink. By the time the dumpster lid had reopened, Max had vowed never to nap in the trash again, no matter how convenient.

And then there was the darkness. In it, everything was suddenly unfamiliar and foreign. He felt small and lonely and unprotected. Just like now.

He began to whine again, louder and louder until he thought his heart would burst with stress and uncertainty and fear.

There was a rustling in the corner, and the light flickered back on. The girl climbed out of bed, rubbing her eyes. She came to Max and sat down in front of his cage. She didn't open the door to let him out, but she did press her hand up to the metal bars, letting Max lift his nose up to her palm to familiarize himself with her scent.

"Hey, Max," the girl said. "I know you're scared. Every time I go somewhere new, I get scared, too." She drew her hand away when Max licked it, her face wrinkling in disgust, but then she put it back.

"I don't know how long we're going to know each other. I've never been in one place longer than nine months, and knowing my luck, I'll get taken out of here just like everywhere else," the girl continued.

"But I'll do my best to make you feel at home here. It's not your fault that your first family was a dud." She frowned. "Giving you up because they were afraid you were going to bite, without you doing anything wrong, makes me so mad. It wasn't right for them to judge you like that."

Listening to the girl's voice made Max feel a little better. He couldn't understand what she was saying, but she was talking to him in a soft voice, and the murder she had in her eyes earlier was completely gone.

"My first foster family was kind of a dud, too," the girl said. "They decided after just three months that having a kid running around was too stressful. Then my second foster family moved across the country and didn't take me. But my third placement, the one before this one—well, I kind of got myself kicked out of it." She bit her lip. "I'm not sorry about it, though."

The girl shook her head quickly, as if trying to brush off the memory. She glanced at the clock. "Anyway, it's bedtime." She lifted the hinges on the cage and opened the door. Max tried to come out, but she pushed him back gently.

"This is your bed," she told him. "You're going to sleep here tonight. But I'll stay here until you fall asleep."

Max pushed against the girl's hand one more time, but when it didn't budge, he sighed and settled into the soft fabric. The girl stroked his head, each pat calming his nervous heartbeat a little bit more, until the whines faded from his throat and he was able to close his eyes and think about sleeping.

He did not drift off until much later, but when he did, he knew that the girl was still with him, her hand on his side, her head half-tucked inside the cage as she curled up next to him, keeping him company while he slept.

CHAPTER 7
EMI

THREE WEEKS LATER, Emi woke to a front paw stepping on her cheek.

"What the—" was all she got out before a back paw landed, by some horrible miracle, inside her mouth.

Emi sat up, spitting dog-foot taste off her tongue and rubbing her neck. She had spent the last twenty-one days on the floor trying to comfort Max, and for the last twenty-one days, he had rewarded her by getting up at the crack of dawn while she was still asleep to pee by her door. This morning, however, he had been kind enough to step on her face, waking her up before his usual routine. As Emi watched, Max's hind leg began to lift up.

"No. No, no, no!" Emi sprang to her feet, already knowing the front door was too far away. She yanked open her window. Frigid air poured into the room as she hooked

Max up to the leash she grabbed from her nightstand. She hauled Max up to the window and looked below. There was an icy snowbank just a foot down, made from dripping icicles along the eaves of the house.

Emi dumped Max over the windowsill, where he landed on all fours. A yellow hole immediately formed beneath him, growing deeper and deeper as he relieved himself. When he was done, Emi tugged on his leash, and he jumped back through the window, tracking wet snow all across her bed.

At least it wasn't pee. Emi rubbed her eyes and brushed off the soft white clumps from her blanket. She got dressed and met Jim and Meili in the kitchen. As he did every Saturday, Jim had made scrambled eggs and toast, and after feeding Max his scoop of dog food, which he finished almost as soon as she was done pouring it into his bowl, Emi settled into her chair to eat.

"So," said Jim as he sat next to her and Meili, who was pouring out glasses of orange juice. "Did Max go inside your room again?"

"Not this morning, for once," Emi said, gulping down half of her OJ. She coughed. "But I don't know how he's going to do today around the house. And we're almost out of carpet cleaner."

"I'll go pick some up today." Jim forked up his eggs and chewed.

Meili touched Emi gently on the shoulder. "Sounds like Max has made some progress on the house-training. How would you feel about teaching him a few tricks?"

"Tricks?" Emi loaded her toast with eggs. She wasn't too big of a fan of how they smelled when they were cooking, but she loved the way they tasted—salty and soft and full of flavor.

"You could teach him how to sit. Stay. Roll over. Play dead." Meili sat down and began to load her own plate of eggs. "Though I'm not a fan of shaking hands. Feels too much like the dog's begging for something."

Emi opened her mouth to tell Meili that shaking hands was exactly what she was going to teach Max, but she was too tired to be snippy. She just wanted to finish breakfast and go back to bed and try to catch up on some sleep.

It had been harder than she had thought to have a dog. Max no longer cried at night, but Emi had lost eight pairs of socks and one sneaker to his chewing habits, as well as every single one of her shoelace tips.

And then there were all the things she had to do when no one was going to be home to limit Max's destruction.

Bathroom doors had to be closed to protect the toilet paper rolls. Shoes had to be stowed. Any food item left on the counter was always at risk of being unexpectedly disappeared.

At the very least, she was becoming more familiar with the house. She knew where to find extra toilet paper now and which cleaning supplies went where.

And, despite having thought that by this time she would have had one big outburst or one mad moment that would have sent her back whirling into the foster care system, she had been too busy taking care of Max to even think about acting out. Emi had thought that she was the one with the task of causing havoc and disruption inside a house—turns out, Max had her beat by a mile.

Whenever Emi came home to a mess or a missing thing, she wanted to be mad at Max. But there was something about him that she couldn't blame him for his actions. Despite his accidents and his chewing, there was a clumsy helplessness to him that made her more sad than angry when she found herself cleaning up after him.

What's more, she found herself worrying about Max when she was at school, knowing that he would be fine in Jim's and Meili's hands (they had had three dogs before Max, all of which had lived long, full lives) but wondering if he was bored or lonely or gnawing away at a forbidden object. Books, boots, hidden Starburst packages—at some point he had chewed through all of them.

When the school bus dropped her off and she went up the driveway to the house, her steps always got a little faster when she would see Max's big head peering out the living room window, his mouth frantically barking as he pawed at the glass.

Emi had been through so many school systems she had given up on needing to fit in. She simply ignored the rare offer to hang out and chose to sit alone at lunch in the big cafeteria.

But here, she was unconsciously beginning to make a routine that felt almost comfortable. After school was milk and cookies at four o'clock and one—only one, no matter how cute his cock-eared begging face looked—Milk-Bone treat for Max, followed by running around the house trying to get Max's energy out with playtime.

Jim and Meili had gotten a few toys for Max. The plushes only lasted a few days before inevitably being torn apart by Max's chewing-machine mouth. But there was a blue-and-yellow braided tug toy that had become part of an everyday ritual between Emi and Max, where she would throw it to him and he would race, full speed, then leap up with his front paws and pounce on it.

Sometimes Max brought it back to Emi; most times he just gnawed at it happily until she went over and wrestled it out of his mouth so she could throw it again.

And then, after playtime, there was homework at the kitchen table next to the soapstone stove, with Max curled around her feet to keep her warm.

And when the grandfather clock in the living room chimed six, Emi would scoop a cup of kibble out and Max would have his dinner. Emi always made sure she wasn't too early or too late. Then, by six thirty, she was at the table with Jim and Meili. She still didn't have much to say to them, but dinners had gotten less awkward every time they talked about Max.

Now Meili was asking Emi if she wanted to teach Max some commands, and although the tip of her tongue was begging her to say that Max deserves to be the wild, untamed beast that he was meant to be, she thought about the strange niceness of rules and boundaries and nodded as she finished her breakfast.

Meili smiled. "I'll pick up some training treats in town today."

"Be sure they're small, and that there are a lot of them," Emi said. "I don't think Max is going to be an easy learner."

When Meili returned with a bag of mini training treats she had picked up from Rite Aid, Emi took it from her and tore it open. The treats were shaped like tiny bones, each one made of peanut butter and oats.

"Want help training him?" Meili asked.

Emi shook her head. "I've watched a bunch of YouTube videos. I know what I'm doing."

"All right." Meili nodded and left the room.

Emi was glad her foster mom hadn't insisted. She wanted to be the only person responsible for Max's education. For as long as she was here, he was her dog. That way, maybe he would always remember her, even if she moved on. Even *when* she moved on, she reminded herself.

She switched on her YouTube video and settled into the living room with Max, who lay on a rug nearby, curled up in a sleepy ball.

"Show the treat to your dog," the YouTube girl with the confident voice instructed. She was holding a treat in front of a fancy-looking, fluffy-faced dog that definitely did not come from the pound and definitely did not have any pit bull in him. "Then move it close to his nose so he can sniff it. Once he does, you move your hand from his nose to his forehead. He'll try to follow your hand with his nose, which will make him lower his rear to the floor. As soon as he does that, give him the treat while saying, 'Sit.' Then repeat until he sits. Simple!"

Five days and 138 treats later, the bag was empty, and Emi was no closer to being able to get Max to sit than when she started. "You're hopeless," she told Max, throwing the bag in the trash. She went to the cupboard and pulled out a Kit Kat. She broke off two of the wafery, chocolaty sticks and sat munching while she shook her head at Max. "You're never going to learn."

Max woofed happily and rolled on his back. His front paws swayed in the air as his back legs splayed onto the carpet.

Emi smiled and finished the rest of the Kit Kat. She knelt down and began to rub Max's tummy. As she did, the front door opened and Meili came into the house, stamping the snow off her boots.

"Hi, Emi. Hi, Max," she said as she took her jacket off and hung it on a wooden coatrack.

"Hey, Meili," Emi said. She bit her lip and swallowed her stubbornness. "On second thought, I thought I might let you help me train Max how to sit."

"Of course!" Meili went to the kitchen and ran her hands under steaming water to warm them. When she was done, she turned off the water and dried her hands on a towel draped across the oven-door handle. "Teaching a dog to sit is kind of like riding a bike. You fail and fail and fail . . . and then one day you get it, and it feels like the beginning of the world. Do you remember how you learned to ride a bicycle?" she asked Emi.

Ride a bicycle. The words poured into Emi's ears, and for a moment, she felt like she was drowning. She knew Meili had asked a straight question, but she still felt memories flooding back to her in a wash of longing and grief.

CHAPTER 8
EMI

SHE HAD BEEN six. The bike had been a Huffy, with silver tassels, pink spokes, pink handlebars, and an ocean of pink hearts on the frame.

It was the best, brightest memory of her mom she had. Before her mom got sick. Before the foster homes.

Emi remembered wheeling the Huffy along the cracked sidewalk outside their rented mobile home. She remembered trying not to run over the dandelions poking through the cement, because dandelions were her mom's favorite flower. *Now, aren't they the most cheerful yellow,* her mom had told her just the day before, when they had gathered a bundle and placed them in an old soda bottle that they had painted using the six colors they had from the Disney princess paint box activity book they had gotten from the dollar bin at Walmart.

Even though the soda bottle had long been recycled, in Emi's mind it had been the most beautiful vase in the world.

She had gotten on the bike and it had immediately tipped, the pedal scraping against her shin and the chain leaving a smear of grease along her calf. Undeterred, she had gotten right back up, only to fall over and over again as she tried to learn to ride that Huffy. Her knees were crisscrossed with bruises and cuts, and the palms of her hands were almost as bad, but she kept getting up and kept on trying because her mom was watching her and she didn't want to let her mom down.

Finally, when Emi had taken a massive spill that left a gash along her elbow the size of a half-used pencil, her mom had helped her up, cleaned her wounds, and then brought her back outside.

Emi had climbed on the bike again, and this time, her mom's hands were on her own, warm and firm, guiding her down the street. That time, Emi had held steady. That time, she had not ridden but flown down the street on her bicycle, her mom's hands like angel wings keeping her aloft.

Now her mom was gone and Meili was asking her to remember. Emi shook her head, clearing the past that had swum across her mind. She was here with Meili and her dog, and she was going to teach her dog how to sit.

"I remember," Emi told Meili. "It's just like that, huh? Simple."

Meili went to the cupboard and took out a new bag of training treats. She tore the plastic strip off the top to open it and picked out a single treat. She handed it to Emi. "Hold this to his nose, but don't let him take it from you," she instructed.

Emi closed a hand around the treat and brought it down to Max. His eyes lit up, and he began to sniff furiously. Emi giggled as Max licked her knuckles.

"What next?" she asked Meili.

"Slowly bring your hand up. When he raises his head, he should sit," said Meili.

Emi drew her hand higher. Max leaped and bonked her hand, causing her to drop the treat. Before she could pick it up, he had ducked his head, and treat 139 was gone.

Meili gave her another treat to try on Max. This time, Max ran in circles around her hand, but his butt never touched the ground.

"How would you feel if I tried?" Meili asked.

Emi thought about it. She wanted to be the one to teach Max, but after so many lost treats, she was willing to try something new. "Sure," she said.

Meili took a treat out. "Max, come," she said as she backed away.

Max sat.

"Huh," said Meili.

Emi bit back a giggle. "Good boy, I think?" she said.

Meili smiled. "Sure," she said, and let Max have the treat. "Your turn," she told Emi.

"Why don't we both try?" Emi asked. She gave Meili a treat and took one for herself. "Maybe we can teach him 'come' and 'sit' at the same time."

She went to one end of the living room while Meili went to the other. Together, they crouched and called to Max as he danced, confused, between the two of them.

An hour, another empty training-treat package, and a number of laughs later, Max was still no closer to learning any commands. But as Emi stood next to Meili at the kitchen sink, watching her foster mother scrub dog slobber off her hands, her breath caught. In the glinting afternoon light, Meili's hair shone with beautiful black brilliance, and her smoke-colored eyes sparkled with a familiar kindness and warmth.

Meili turned from the sink and noticed Emi's gaze.

"What is it?" she asked.

"I was just . . . thinking about my mom," Emi said. She paused, then went on. "I'm glad to be here. With you."

Meili nodded. "Me too, Emi." She turned off the faucet and faced Emi. "Maine's about as white a state as you can get. So for you and me, it can be tough. I know we talked about it a little when you first arrived—how it feels to look different from everyone around you, and how it can weigh on you."

Emi slid a hand towel off the oven handle. "Yeah. Sometimes it feels like everyone's staring at me in school. Or at the grocery store. Or anywhere, really." She handed the towel to Meili.

"You feel watched. Like people are expecting you to behave differently because you're not white. Or that you have to prove that you belong." Meili dried her hands, then held the towel ready while Emi washed her hands.

When Emi was done, Meili wove the towel around her hands and clasped them tight. She looked straight into Emi's eyes. "I know it can be hard sometimes, being judged as an outsider by how you look. I won't say it's fair or right. But I am here for you. I know what you're going through, and if you need to talk anytime, you just let me know. Okay?"

Emi felt her foster mother's hands clasping hers, firm and steady. She hesitated, then pressed back once, lightly. "Okay," she said.

"Good." Meili gave Emi's hands a final squeeze, then unwrapped them and draped the towel across the oven handle. "Now, let's see about getting Max another bag of training snacks. Though I think he may be faking it, that little treat gobbler."

She arched an eyebrow at Emi, and they both started chuckling, and Emi felt a quiet happiness she hadn't felt in a long time.

It wasn't a handful of dandelions in a bottle, but it would have to do.

CHAPTER 9
MAX

Max's Guide to Getting So Many Treats

1. Spend days with the girl eating lots and lots of yummy treats that she seems to give you while making the same noise with her mouth over and over.

2. Halfway through the third week, wonder if the mouth noise the girl makes actually might mean something.

3. Sit to think about it.

4. See the girl's face light up.

5. Dismiss thought and go back to accepting treat after treat while running around the girl and wagging tail.

6. See the girl's face fall.

7. Get dizzy from running around the girl and sit.

8. See the girl's face light up.

9. Wonder why the girl still makes the same noise whenever you sit.

10. Remain confused, two weeks and hundreds of treats later.

One morning, the girl slung a backpack over her shoulder and called to Max while standing at the front door. As she got his leash and collar, Max pranced around her, barking and woofing. It was outside time!

"Sit," the girl commanded.

Max whined and pawed at the door.

"Sit," the girl said again.

There was that same noise again. Max cocked his head, then went back to pawing the door, a happy, anxious whine in his throat.

The girl sighed and bent over him, fastening the collar

around his neck. When she opened the door, he trotted out, straining at his leash like he always did.

The girl led him into the woods. Max sniffed at everything, tugging her right and left like a windshield wiper on its fastest setting.

When they had gone far enough so that nothing else surrounded them except for the woods, the girl stopped. She opened her backpack and immediately Max was alert. He smelled something faintly. Something good.

The girl pulled out the bag of dog treats. She opened it, and Max's saliva glands went into overdrive as the smell of salt and meat hit him. He barked at the girl hopefully.

The girl held up a treat. She shook her head as Max leaped up to grab it. She enclosed the treat in her fist and lifted it above his head.

Max whined, frustrated. "Sit," the girl said firmly, and opened her hand. Max greedily licked the treat off her hand and crunched down on it. It was delicious.

The girl held out another treat. "Sit," she said again.

Max wagged his tail.

"Sit," repeated the girl.

Max wagged his tail harder.

"Sit," said the girl in a tired voice.

Max was also getting tired. He folded his hind legs and sat.

The girl let out a surprised yelp. She lifted her hands in a wild burst of triumph, then grabbed Max and smothered him in a giant hug. She patted his nose and fed him the treat. "Good boy," she said. "Good, good boy. You're listening. I can trust you!"

Her hand went to his collar. There was a little click of the leash's metal unclipping, and suddenly Max found himself free.

He made one unbelieving circle around the girl. Then he sprang forward, and back and right and left and sideways. He galloped ahead, barking joyfully.

"Max!"

Max turned his head. His legs ached to go forward, but he saw something in the girl's hand. It was another treat.

"Come," she said.

Max bounded back to her and gobbled down the treat. He licked the girl's hand and woofed happily. The girl drew his face into the warmth of her chest and gently stroked his back. For a moment, Max felt a curious kind of attachment to the girl.

But then, as the girl straightened to her feet, he realized that there was no leash holding him back. He could go anywhere!

His instinct to try escape attempt #11 overwhelmed him,

and before he could properly think, he had bolted. Ignoring the girl's cries, Max fled through the woods, heady with the speed of freedom as he crested a hill and disappeared from the girl's view. He continued to run, delirious with the raw joy as her voice got fainter and fainter.

When he finally stopped, he could hear nothing. The forest surrounded him, full of possibility. He could go in any direction for however far he wanted. He was free. He barked and howled his joy to the silent trees.

As the morning deepened into afternoon, Max made his way farther into the woods, his initial elation falling away as he felt the cold of the still-iced ground seeping through his paws. When he reached a sunlit field bordered by a crumbling stone wall that had dried of snow, he hopped on top of the wall and curled up for a nap.

When he awoke, the sun had moved off the wall, and he was freezing. The bottoms of his paws had turned into ice. Max chewed off the ice chunks and licked his paws until they were warm. By the time he was done, he was shivering. He had to get moving.

He jumped off the wall, and a rumble of hunger curled in his belly. He was beginning to regret leaving the girl and her bag full of snacks.

CHAPTER 10
EMI

"HELP!" EMI HAD backtracked through the woods and had reached the edge of the driveway, shouting before she had even made it into the house. "Jim! Meili! Somebody help!"

A moment later, Jim opened the door, his woolen socks scratching against the welcome mat. "Emi? What's wrong?"

"Max! He . . . he . . ." Emi's heart was hammering so hard she felt like it would beat its way out of her chest. "He got away in the woods and I can't find him and I don't know what to do."

Jim nodded. "Okay. Come inside. Warm up. I'm going to get some things together, and then we'll go out looking for him."

Emi pushed down the panic that was rising in her throat and hurried into the house. She looked down at the leash in her hands. She was clutching the metal clasp so hard it was leaving an imprint in her palm. She wanted to be so angry at Max. She had trusted him, and he had broken her trust. It was all his fault.

Only it wasn't. Emi bit her lip and shook her head, trying to dash away her thought, but it came all the same. It was her fault. Max didn't know any better. Whatever happened to him, out there in the woods, would be all her fault.

Jim was suddenly in front of her, a backpack hitched to his shoulders, pulling on his snow boots. "Just have to lace these up, and I'll be ready to track Max down with you," he said.

Emi glanced at the slanted afternoon light shimmering through the trees. In a few hours, it would be dark. "What if we can't find him, Jim? What if he doesn't come back and has to spend the night in the woods?"

"We'll find him," Jim replied. There was a certainty in his voice, a steel drop of determination, that Emi had never heard before. He finished tying his boots and stood up. "Let's go."

Emi followed Jim out the door. The guilt and anxiety curdling in her stomach made her want to throw up. But watching her foster father stride down the steps with his straight back and sure steps lent her a flicker of hope. That Jim would know what to do. That he would make it better.

For the first time since she had entered the foster system, Emi felt like she could put her trust in someone. It was as if an invisible thread of connection had formed in her chest and reached out from her to attach to her foster dad. It was only a single strand, fragile as the delicate icicles hanging from the eaves, but it was there.

She hurried over to Jim's side and pointed into the opening in the woods where she had led Max. "Let me show you where he ran off."

The place where Max had run off still had snow across the ground. Emi pointed to the direction Max had escaped, and Jim knelt down, scanning the white ground, until he pointed to a set of tracks in the snow. "Got them," he said.

As Jim tracked, Emi followed him. They bushwhacked through broken pines and scrub, calling for Max constantly, ducking under branches and squeezing through openings between bushes that clawed at their jackets, but which Max wouldn't have had any trouble navigating.

The tracks led on and on. When the last of daylight started slipping behind the horizon, Jim pulled two flashlights from his backpack and handed one to Emi. "Do you want to keep looking or go home?" he asked her.

She was starting to get tired, but she wasn't going to give up. "Keep going," Emi said, switching on the light. Her mittens and socks were keeping her warm, and she didn't want to think about how she would feel if she didn't find Max that night.

Night came, then deep night, and still the tracks didn't lead to Max. Emi felt her heart twist each time they came to an opening in the thick woods and she called for her dog, hoping to see him emerge in the moonlight and run toward her, an ending fit for a cheesy G-rated movie, but he didn't appear.

On they went, weaving across the cold, dark landscape, until Max's pawprints led them abruptly to the road.

Jim turned to Emi and shook his head. "Looks like he made it at least two miles from home. I'll call Meili and have her come get us." As he reached for his phone, he patted Emi on the shoulder. "We've done all we can tonight. Best to head on home, and we'll pick up where we left and search for him at first light tomorrow."

"Do you think he'll be okay?" Emi asked.

"He's a smart dog. I bet he's found a cozy little den for

himself," Jim said. "Or maybe he's made it to some neighbor's shed. We can ask around in the morning." Pulling his fingers out of his gloves, he made a call, and a few minutes later the gray pickup's headlights flashed out along the road.

Meili welcomed Emi into the truck with a thermos of hot chocolate and a hug. When they got home, she fed Emi soup and showed her a Missing poster she had created on her laptop while Emi and Jim had searched for Max.

"Hopefully Max will come home tomorrow, but just in case, we'll put these up around the neighborhood—that way, if any of our neighbors see him, they'll know to call us," she told Emi.

"Thanks, Meili." Emi blinked. "I . . . I really appreciate you doing this for Max." She turned to Jim. "You too."

"We know how much he means to you," Meili replied. She folded down her computer and cleared Emi's bowl. "I'll clean up. You get some sleep now, okay?"

As Emi nodded, she felt like something tight and hard in her chest was starting to melt. Her foster parents hadn't yelled at her once for losing Max. In fact, they were doing everything they could to help her. They were on her side, and it meant a lot.

She went to the bathroom to brush her teeth. After getting into her pajamas and crawling into bed, she tried to close her eyes and drift off.

But sleep didn't come. She kept picturing Max out in the cold, scared and lonely and hungry. He had missed six-o'clock dinner. He had never missed six-o'clock dinner.

And it wasn't just him missing his food—Emi missed feeding him. She had missed that part of their ritual, and it felt like a piece of her routine that had started to give her comfort was suddenly gone, snapped and broken by this horrible thing that had happened.

She wanted it back. More than anything she wanted that stupid, simple task of scooping kibble into Max's bowl at his hour. At *their* hour.

It was no use trying to sleep. She got up and went out to the living room, where she got a chair and moved it to the front door. She settled herself in to wait, straining her ears to hear the whisper of a bark or a scratch at the door. And there she sat, twisting her jade bracelet, staring at the small patch of light the outdoor bulb gave off until dawn.

CHAPTER 11
RED

RED LOVED THE night. She loved the silky quiet of it, the way her ears could pick up the twitches of mouse whiskers in the darkness, in the near silence. She loved stalking her prey with practiced, measured steps—the pounce, the kill, the feast.

She had spent the past few hours combing her territory— a two-mile-wide stretch of pine and scrub—for dinner and had found not one but two mice that had made a squeaking, delicious meal, and she was ready to retire to the shed.

As she passed the house, she paused. There was a light on inside. Red knew the habits of the humans who lived within. They were never up at that hour.

Through the glass, she saw the face of the girl. Her face was pale, and there were dark smudges under her eyes.

She looked like she would collapse at any second. But her gaze was fixed on the woods with a peculiar sort of intensity.

Red turned her head back toward the woods. She saw nothing that would interest the girl. When she turned back, the woman had come over to the girl, dressed in a robe, her hair tousled from sleep.

The woman spoke to the girl. The girl shook her head fiercely. The woman spoke again, and Red saw the girl's face soften. She stood up from the chair she had been sitting on and stumbled. The woman caught her, scooped her up, and moved away from the window.

A minute later, the woman came back and settled herself on the chair where the girl had been, her eyes trained on the woods.

Something had happened. Or, something was happening. Red, full of mouse and lazily curious, jumped up on her familiar stone wall perch to watch.

An hour later, as the sun was rising, the man, holding two mugs, appeared in the window. He gave a mug to the woman, who kissed him on the cheek and drank from it gratefully. They talked, both of them looking toward the woods. Then the man got into his thick clothes and left the house, heading into the woods.

A few hours later, the woman and the girl left, too. Only, instead of heading into the woods, they went to the end of the driveway and stopped in front of a telephone pole by the main road. The girl was holding a stack of papers, the woman, a stapler. The girl pressed one of the papers on the telephone pole while the woman stapled it in place. They continued down the road, putting a piece of paper on every telephone pole until they had disappeared from view.

Curious to see what they were doing, Red walked up to one of the pieces of paper. On it she saw Max's face.

Max. Come to think of it, she hadn't seen the girl take him outside the house all morning. Red was used to being woken up from her morning nap by Max's excited barking, but today something was different.

Red twitched her tail. It wasn't just that something was different. Something was wrong. Even though she had spent a full night hunting and would normally be curled up in the shed by now, she was unnerved by the strange actions of the humans.

And when it took hours for the girl and the woman to come home, and hours after that for the man to appear, his face tight and drawn as he emerged from the woods alone as evening fell and still there was no Max peeing around the house, then Red understood what was happening.

Max was lost. The foolish, ill-built for winter with his short fur, clueless about what it took to survive, brick of a dog had somehow gotten himself out of the house, mistaking flight for freedom, and now Red had serious doubts that he would find his way back to the warmth of the house again.

She felt a flicker of pity. She did not tolerate weakness in herself, but even though Max was almost as helpless as a newborn kitten, he amused her. She would have liked to have been entertained by his floppy paws and wobbly head just a little longer before he was swallowed by the woods.

The next day, Max still hadn't returned. Red woke from her afternoon nap to the smell of frying meat. The man had hauled a grill into the driveway and was cooking burgers. When the girl came home from school, she and the man took the burgers and went into the woods.

Red, curious to see what they were doing with the morsels of meat, followed them. When they had gotten to a spot dotted with old pawprints, the girl dropped a hamburger at the foot of a tree. They went through the woods, stopping every so often to nestle another burger by a stream or under the roots of a tipped-over tree.

Red knew what they were doing. The stream was a necessary resource for a dog—water. The upturned tree, a potential den. If Max was alive, they were trying to feed him.

That didn't stop Red from taking a nibble or two from the burgers they placed. But she was careful not to eat the whole thing. She could hunt. She could survive on her own.

Max couldn't.

On the third day, Red pushed through her natural instinct to nestle inside the shed and doze, and went into the woods to find Max.

It wasn't as though they were friends. And Max, if she thought about it hard, was really of no use to her.

But she couldn't get the memory of the girl's face out of her head from three nights ago. Sad. Searching. Caught in the predawn light between hope and despair.

Despite herself, Red wanted to help the girl. So she

forwent her traditional afternoon nap and put her hunting skills to work.

Max's tracks were all over the woods. She sniffed until she found ones that seemed to be the freshest. As the sun sank and rose again, she followed his tracks patiently, relentlessly, ignoring the hunger in her belly as she crisscrossed through the frozen brush, over mountains and hills, across streams and valleys, until it seemed as though the world had become nothing but scent, pawprints, and trail.

She did not sleep, and she did not lose track of where she was.

Finally, as dusk was beginning to fall, she crested a hill and saw him. He was fifty feet below, lapping water from a river, ribs straining against his sides, as thin as autumn grass.

Red went down to him. "Max," she said.

Max yelped. "Red? How did you . . . ? What are you . . . ? Where did you . . . ? Do you have any food?"

Red sighed. "No, but I know where you can find some. Follow me." She turned her tail and headed back toward the area where the girl had dropped the hamburgers.

As she went, she heard Max following her. When he uttered a short whimper, she looked back. He was limping.

"What did you do?" Red asked.

"I fell in a hole funny," Max said. He hopped forward. "But I'll be okay."

"Well, then, keep up," Red said gruffly. She turned and kept going but slowed down a little so Max didn't have to hurry on his injured leg to stay with her.

"You know, freedom isn't as great as I thought it would be," Max said as they moved through the woods. "I thought everything would be perfect as soon as I escaped. But it's not."

"Freedom is responsibility," Red replied. "It's work. And you aren't ready to handle it."

"But . . ."

"Listen," Red said. "You're hungry. You're hurt. You're cold. And you're too dumb to realize what you've got."

"What's that?" asked Max.

"A little girl who loves you," said Red. "I watched her wait for you when you didn't come home. I watched her search for you, put out food for you that I'm leading you to right now, lose sleep over you. She's worth more than your freedom. She *is* your freedom. You're just too bent on what you think freedom is to actually recognize it."

They had reached the hamburgers. After Max wolfed

down the frozen bites, Red led him straight on a direct path back to the house.

When they reached it, Red nudged Max toward the door. "Go now," she told him. "Go inside. Get warm. And do whatever ridiculous dog things you do to tell the girl you're thankful. She deserves it."

CHAPTER 12
MAX

Max's Guide to a Strange New Feeling

1. See a pile of more hamburger under the front porch. Also see lots of treats. And a blanket and bed—*your* blanket and bed! You can tell by the way they stink. It is a comforting smell.

2. Eat hamburger.

3. Circle eighteen times around bed. Make self dizzy.

4. Lie down.

5. Hear door open above you. Then hear sound of shoes coming down steps.

6. See the girl's face.

7. Lick it.

8. Feel, for the first time, like you belong.

Early morning a week later, Max woke up in the girl's bedroom, nestled at the foot of her bed. He could hear her breath, soft and even. She was still asleep.

He yawned and stretched, then walked onto the girl and thumped down on her chest. He pushed his nose into her face.

"Max," the girl murmured, sleepily batting him away. "It's not time yet."

Max pawed at the girl's nose. She giggled and turned on her side, spilling him over next to her. He landed on his side and kept going until he was on his back, legs dangling, paws waving.

"All right, all right," the girl said, leaning over and giving him a belly scratch.

Since coming back, their routine had changed. The girl allowed him on her bed now, and often he would fall asleep to her arm wrapped around him. She spent more time with him, talked to him, had been patient as he hopped around on three legs until the pain in his fourth one had subsided, and was there to play tug-of-war with him when he had finally recovered.

Before, the girl had been a dispenser of food, a water bowl filler, a door opener. She had been a strange creature who gave him what he needed to live, but he had not really paid attention to her.

But after she had saved him, after Red had told him about what the girl had done to get him back, the girl had become something different to Max. Instead of fighting her on the leash, he began to worry about her. He felt an explosion of joy when she looked at him and smiled.

He liked to make her laugh.

He began to notice things about her. How her silky, jet-black hair smelled like coconut and lemon. How her ear scratches became deeper and longer the more she got to know him. How she liked to run a hand down his back before rubbing the patch of fur just above his tail, smiling as his tail rose and wagged automatically. How she hugged him tightly but never too tightly.

He had been content to be at the center of her attention. Now she was the center of his.

When the girl left the house without him, Max didn't feel quite right until she came back. The older man and the kind woman would sometimes pat him every so often, but their hands did not give him the same sense of contentedness as the girl's.

The girl held on to his leash with an iron grip when he went outside. But there was a day, when the snow had melted to a dusting on the ground and new bright green blades of grass had started poking out of the ground, when a little wasp flew up into the girl's face and the girl brought both hands up to defend herself, dropping the leash.

Max looked at the leash.

He looked at the girl.

He looked at the leash.

He looked at the girl, who no longer had the wasp buzzing around her eyes.

He picked up the leash in his mouth and handed it to the girl.

The girl took the leash from Max. A moment later, she was on her knee, wrapping him in a warm, tight hug.

"Well, look at that," a voice called from the stone wall.

Max turned his head. Red was staring at him with a curl

of amusement on her lips. She was grooming her paw but had stopped to watch.

"Look at what?" Max woofed.

"You've finally got some sense in your fuzzy big head," replied Red. "You're not running away."

"My head's not fuzzy," Max said.

Red ignored him. "I don't know how much sense that girl's got, but however much she has, it's more than you. You keep her close. Stay loyal to her, and she'll stay loyal to you."

"You think so?" Max asked.

Red shrugged. "Judging from the way she's looking at you right now, there's no way that she would ever leave you."

"She wouldn't leave me," Max said.

But there was something that rang wrong in his ears, even after they had gone back inside and the girl had sat at the table and warmed her feet against his belly as he stretched out under the kitchen table. He remembered the family he had been part of before the girl and the man and the woman.

Before them, there had been just a man and a woman. They had done many of the same things the girl and her family had done, and Max had loved them, and he thought they had loved him back. But sometime after the first year he had been with them, the woman's belly had grown bigger and bigger, and she had looked at him with sadder and sadder eyes.

Then one day the man had loaded him in the car and driven to the animal shelter. The slam of the car door behind Max was a sound he could still sometimes hear. The man had dropped him off at the animal shelter without even a final hug.

Max hadn't known what he had done wrong. He had been the best he could be, and somehow he had ended up back at the shelter, homeless and without a family. And even the kindest shelter worker couldn't fill the emptiness in his heart. He didn't know where he belonged there. He had no pack. He had no place.

Here, with this girl, he had both.

A few months later, Max was tracking mud into the kitchen after a spring romp in the backyard when he noticed something. The woman, who was usually skinny as a stick, was starting to swell around her middle. There was a small bump along her midsection that filled Max with unease, though he couldn't pinpoint why.

MEILI WAS SERVING lamb stew that night. Emi loved its richness, the fat of the lamb melding with the thick starchiness of the potatoes, with peas bobbing around, little green globes of unexpected sweetness. She had never had a foster mom who could cook so well, and she had even begun to cut back on the SweeTARTS and jelly beans she would buy at the middle school concessions store with the five-dollar allowance she was given every week. She found herself wanting to be hungry for dinner.

"So, how was school today?" Jim asked as they all settled around the table.

"It was . . . good!" Emi picked up her spoon and dug in. She ate a bite, swallowed, and continued, "Mrs. Adelman brought in a dozen roses for us today in homeroom. She told us it was to remind us that even though the winter's been really long this year, it will eventually end. She even let us smell them!"

"What did they smell like?" Meili asked, smiling.

"Soft. Sweet. Like . . . summer," Emi said. "Plus, there was a bug in one of them."

Jim laughed. "That's part of summer, too. Flies, no-see'ums, and mosquitoes. But you've also got garden days, river swims, and bike rides, too."

"I'm excited." Emi wolfed down another spoonful of stew and kept going. "Today, a girl sat with me at lunch. Her name's Candace. Her family just moved here, and she doesn't know anybody. I like her. We talked about movies and our favorite lines from them. I was thinking that maybe she could come over one day."

"That would be great," said Meili. "You just let me know when, and I'll bake treats."

Max, who was curled at Emi's feet, woofed.

Emi grinned down at him. "The treats aren't for you, buddy. But good try."

Max still hadn't learned "sit" yet. But it hadn't been hard to teach him "treat."

The thought of eating snacks with a new friend in the house filled Emi with a strange kind of hope. Over the past couple of months, she had really opened up to Jim and Meili. Started saying more than just "Pass the salt" at the dinner table. She had begun to tell them about talks with her case worker, Ms. Lindner, who had just told her yesterday that she could see how well Emi was starting to fit in. To belong.

It had all started when Max had run away. Emi had been devasted, hadn't known what to do but to stare out the window and wait for him and worry and think about what an idiot she had been to let him go. She hadn't known what to do, and she had felt so utterly helpless.

And then Jim and Meili had swooped in and showed her how to move instead of rage and grieve. How to search for him in the woods, with a backpack filled with warm clothes, food, hot cocoa, and flashlights. How to pin Missing posters on every telephone pole for five miles. How to dash into the truck when a neighbor called with a sighting, and search and search and search. How to lay out hamburgers and soft, familiar bedding.

And even though none of it made a difference in the end, since Max had come back on his own, Jim and Meili had showed Emi that she could take charge of the situation.

Now she looked at the two of them in the warm glow of the soft kitchen light, steam rising from their bowls, and something in her felt like it was cracking open. She hadn't had control of her life for so long, and they were teaching her how to take it. She thought about what it would be like to trust them. To be vulnerable around them.

"Emi, we have something important to tell you," Meili said. She gave Emi a measured look over her bowl of stew. Her tone sounded strange. It was a mix of excitement and something else.

Emi paused, her spoon lifted halfway to her mouth. Her heart leaped into her throat. She had been waiting for that tone, for what it might mean. That she could finally stop feeling that awful sense of uncertainty. That a family wanted her for good, that she was worthy of belonging somewhere.

"What is it?" Emi asked. She tried not to sound too eager for the words she had been waiting to hear for the past two years.

"I'm pregnant," said Meili.

The lamb stew, which Emi had loved and requested over and over during the past five months, suddenly tasted of ash.

Pregnant. A baby. A child that would be loved and wanted from the very beginning. A child that would be so much more important to Jim and Meili than her, a dumb foster kid who was probably just a way for them to practice their parenting skills before dumping her for a kid of their own. Great.

"When are you due?" Emi asked, each word as delicate as broken glass.

"December," said Meili, giving Jim a quiet glance.

Jim cleared his throat. "We've been trying for almost five years to have a baby. We had pretty much given up, but Meili recently found out today that she's carrying, and we wanted you to be the first one to know."

Meili nodded. "And it's early yet. There's a chance something might go wrong. But it's the first time we've been able to conceive."

A piece of lamb stuck in Emi's throat. She felt as though the world was suddenly squeezing her, taking the breath and the hope out of her lungs. Living with Jim and Meili had been the best home she had had since her mom had died. But with their own baby, she knew that she couldn't hope for adoption. They would give her up, just like they had agreed to when they signed her foster papers.

The feelings she had at the beginning of dinner disappeared, leaving a cold, hard knot in her throat.

"I'm so happy for you," said Emi. "May I be excused?" She pushed her chair away from the table and stood up.

"Emi, wait," said Jim. "I know what you're thinking."

"Don't tell me you know me," said Emi, her voice rising. "You have no idea what I'm thinking. Or how I feel. You haven't been bounced around from house to house for the past two years, each time thinking that maybe this time, maybe this time I'll get to stay. Maybe your news is good to you. But to me, it's not."

"Emi," said Meili. Her hand gripped her stew spoon so hard Emi could see the whites of her knuckles. "We thought this would be exciting news for you, too. Because—"

"It's not exciting," Emi said, hating how thin and brittle her voice had become. "It just means that you're going to leave me, like everybody else." She shoved her chair, and it tipped, hitting the wooden floor with a sharp crack.

Before Jim or Meili could speak again, Emi ran past them to her bedroom, slamming the door as hard as she could.

A few minutes later, Max was scratching to be let in. She cracked the door just wide enough to let him squeeze through, then closed the door again. Max hopped onto her bed and sprawled out. He widened his mouth into a yawn, and Emi saw his teeth, stained and slightly crooked, and what they could mean to Jim and Meili's new baby.

Max's old family had given him up because of a newborn. Emi knew that once the kid was born, Jim and Meili's loyalty would be to the baby and not to Max. Not to her, either. Both of them would be yesterday's news come next winter.

She dropped onto the bed and curled herself around Max, feeling his rough fur against her fingers and his comforting warmth against her chest. She would never abandon him. She would be loyal to him. She couldn't trust humans, but she could trust him.

"No matter what happens to me, I won't leave you," she whispered to Max. "Not ever. No matter what, we're sticking together."

She went to bed without brushing her teeth or changing into her pajamas. When she heard a soft knock at her door, she ignored it. She turned to face the wall, her arms crossed as if she were trying to keep her chest from falling apart, thinking.

As the sun faded from her window and the outside woods turned to shadow, Emi kept her arms curled around Max and thought and thought. Finally, when even the crickets had stopped chirping and the sounds inside the house had settled into quiet, Emi got off the bed, patting Max's snoring head before slipping out the bedroom door with her backpack and a flashlight.

An hour later, she returned. Her backpack was full of candy bars, sandwiches, a water bottle filled to the brim, a box of matches, and two gallon-size Ziplocs, one filled with dog kibble and the other with Milk-Bone treats. She packed a few things in the small space that was left—an extra long-sleeved shirt, two pairs of socks, three pairs of underwear, and her hat, then heaved the bag over to the foot of her bed and set an alarm for four the next morning.

Jim and Meili had taught her that she was not helpless. That she could take control of her life. She was going to do it now, for her and for Max. She would take them into the woods, far enough away that they would be hard to track, and she would find a place where they could stay for a couple of days, relying on only themselves. She would find a cave to camp out in, or build herself a tent with branches and leaves. But no matter where she went, she wanted it to be her place. Her decision.

Emi knew it wouldn't be forever. Eventually, she knew she would have to return back to civilization. But it would be a practice run for when she would go away for real, finally saying so long and good riddance to all the adults who had let her down, and the system that was teaching her that she was not worthy of belonging to one place or one family.

She looked down at the dog snoring at her feet. He lay sprawled out, legs bent at angles that couldn't possibly be comfortable but somehow were to him.

Emi reached over and touched the top of Max's head, her fingers curling in an automatic ear scratch. She and Max would be their own family, just the two of them. They would trust no one else, set up concrete walls between themselves and the rest of the world because it was safer that way.

Because trusting others only led to disappointment.

CHAPTER 14
MAX

Max's Guide to Having a Pretty Good Idea That Something Weird Is Happening

1. Be having a really good dream about chasing bunny rabbits and catching them by their funny fluffy tails.

2. Be woken up by the girl.

3. Yawn.

4. Stretch.

5. Sneeze.

6. Notice, *Hey, it's still kind of dark outside.*

7. Yawn again.

8. Get ready for the day. After four months together, you know the routine: accept head pats, look at slippers that girl puts on and drool (one day you will eat them, you promise to yourself), wait to eat while the girl gets out of bed and picks clothes, keep waiting while she does stuff in the bathroom, wait some more as she does more things in the bedroom, then head to the kitchen for . . . BREAKFAST!!!!

9. Realize that something feels off. That you are always ravenous in the morning, but for some reason you don't feel *too* ravenous.

10. Also realize that the girl is not wearing slippers. Instead, she is putting on a pair of boots.

11. Also *also* realize that the girl is fully dressed. And wearing a backpack.

12. Have a vague memory that the girl was filling it the night before but can't remember with what.

13. Momentarily forget that things feel weird when the girl feeds you . . . BREAKFAST!!!!

14. Gobble food. Lick bowl. This part feels familiar.

15. Wag tail.

16. When the girl puts leash on you and brings you outside and starts walking into the woods, realize that this is going to be a very different day indeed. It's going to be an ADVENTURE!

17. (You think.)

They walked for a long time. Max ran ahead of her, sniffing at trees and roots and rocks and all manner of animal poop. He loved the smells that surrounded him. After a winter of almost nothingness, everything had a delicious odor to it—rot and dirt and ooze and slime and the abundance of smells that signaled the full-on headiness of late spring.

The girl did not seem to feel the joy of the energy bursting from the woods, even when he brought her a delicious bug-eaten stick and pushed it into her hand. Instead, she plodded, her boots squelching in the mud, her mouth set in a thin, determined line.

There was no trail. Max didn't mind—he liked to explore all the forest, and because he was low to the ground, there weren't that many overhanging branches to thump his head or get in the way, but as the girl bushwhacked through stubby pines and scratchy bushes, her pace slowed more and more.

It also didn't help the girl that without a trail, it was harder for her to keep ahold of him. Max liked to move left and right, trying to breathe in all the smells of the forest—the wet brown pine needles, thawing dirt, worms, bugs, rotten tree trunks, and new leaves stretching out in the sharp morning air—it was all so good! But as he did, the leash that the girl kept firmly clamped in her hand kept getting twisted up on trees, scrub, stumps, even Max's own legs.

Finally, after untangling Max for what must have been the hundredth time, the girl stopped. She reached into her backpack and pulled out the bag full of dog treats.

Max's mouth began to water as the smell of salt and meat hit him. He barked and circled the girl hopefully.

The girl held out the treat. "Let's see if I can get you to behave a little better," she said. "Sit."

Max woofed and whined.

"Sit?" the girl pleaded.

Max spotted a puddle next to him and decided to roll in it.

"Okay, Max, okay," the girl said, shaking her head. She sighed and then fed him the treat.

As the girl turned to put away the bag of treats, Max saw a flash of slate and gold, black beady eyes, a fluff of tail.

Squirrel. The first squirrel of spring.

The forest seemed to dissolve before Max—the trees, the bushes, the mud all disintegrating into background splashes of color. All he could see was the squirrel scampering head-first down the giant oak twenty feet away, its tiny black claws clinging to the rough bark of the tree. He could see its whiskers and the fragile tufts of fur that clung to the edges of its ears. He could see the muscles flexing beneath its fur, taut and lean from a long winter. And he could see the white belly, soft and juicy.

Suddenly, a ribbon of saliva dropped from Max's mouth. He gave a howl and sprang forward, his legs bounding like a rabbit's as he raced toward his afternoon snack.

The force of his body yanked the leash out of the girl's hand. Max didn't notice. He was too focused on his potential prey.

If the squirrel had turned tail and fled up the tree, everything would have been different. Max would have barked fruitlessly at it while it chittered at him, a safe twenty feet up. Then he would have returned to the girl.

But the squirrel did not go up. Instead, it plunged headlong to the ground and began a desperate sprint across the forest floor.

As Max bolted after it, he felt the power of his legs carrying him forward. There was no leash to pull him back. He didn't even hear the girl's cries as he continued to run, cresting a hill and flying through the muddy woods as her voice got fainter and fainter.

Max did not know how long he chased the squirrel. He only knew that when he stopped, he had burs in his coat and scratches on the pads of his feet, and that he was on a rocky outcropping on the mountain.

Where is my collar? Where is my leash? Max wondered. A fuzzy memory swam back to him from the previous hour—of the leash catching around a tree and him tugging so hard that his collar came off, before continuing to chase the squirrel.

When the trees and the forest fell back into place, he looked around and realized he had never been to this part of the woods before. He had no idea where he was, or how he had gotten there. He climbed up onto a boulder to see if he could spot anything familiar. There was nothing. He was lost.

Not again, Max, he thought. *Actually, not again . . . again.*

Max started to climb down, then stopped. Far down below, he saw something near the shore of a wide ribbon of river. He couldn't be sure, but the shadow it cast seemed girl-size.

Hope flooded through him. He leaped, tumbled off the boulder, and ran pell-mell through the trees, trusting his instinct to keep him oriented in the right direction. He heard the sound of snapping branches around him, raking and clawing at him as they left scratches under his belly and along his sides. He did not care.

When he saw a riverbank up ahead, he ran to it, barking with quick, happy ruffs, relieved to have been right. He reached the edge and stopped. The river was wider than he had thought. And loud, with fast-moving water.

But on the other side, he saw the girl. His girl!

Without thinking, Max plunged in and paddled desperately for the far shore. The river swirled and rumbled around him, a monster eager to swallow him whole if he would let it.

Max did not let it. Pulling his body across the fierce current, he made it to the other side. He got out and shook off a gallon of water, then ran to the girl.

But it wasn't a girl. It was just a pile of rocks casting a shadow that was girl-size.

A spike of fear shot through Max's heart. He was lost—really lost now. He did not know where the girl was. And he had no way of knowing how to get back to safety.

CHAPTER 15
RED

THE MICE WERE gone. Red studied the holes in the shed boards where they normally scampered through. During winter, they had appeared, finding shelter from the punishing cold outside. She had greeted them with open paws and a hungry mouth. But with the warming weather, they had left her den of bones to seek homes within the muddy spring fields and ancient stone walls that once divided pasture lands between neighbors.

After another hour of crouching and staring at the empty shed holes, Red's belly was still gurgling. She rose and stretched her stiffened muscles, then slipped outside to go hunting.

She spent the night prowling in the woods, waiting for the familiar pattering of mouse feet to guide her to her midnight snacks. After three successful pounces, she was ready to go inside for a morning nap.

As she approached the house, she saw the girl open the door, a backpack slung around her shoulders and the dog at her side. Red had never seen her leave so early, before proper light had even reached the woods. She shrugged and flicked her tail at Max before going inside the shed and curling up to sleep. As she nuzzled her head into the warmth of her belly, she sensed something was wrong, but she couldn't figure out what, so she closed her eyes and tumbled into sleep.

She awoke to the man and the woman calling for the girl. Bright midmorning light spilled into the shed in long golden slants, illuminating the specks of dust floating in the air. Red stretched and went outside. The man was standing with the front door open, his voice growing increasingly louder. She could see the woman through the window searching inside the house, over and over again, as though the girl would suddenly appear from a hidden spot that she had not seen.

Red walked into the backyard. A quick scan showed her the girl and Max were nowhere close. She would have heard his excited bark.

She loped off in the direction she had seen the two of them going in the morning. Her steps were unhurried as she traced the faint outline of Max's paws in the mud, as well as the girl's own boot prints. Their tracks led deeper and deeper into the woods, until they were past the familiar terrain that Red had carefully mapped throughout her hunts.

Red thought for a moment. She knew the girl could take care of Max, and that she could take care of herself, too. Even though they could be out frolicking in the woods, Red's instincts were telling her that something was unusual—but she couldn't pinpoint it. Maybe not dangerous, but unusual.

She had no obligation to track down the girl and Max. But it was spring, the air was warm, and she had nothing better to do. And if they were in trouble, they would need an experienced set of paws.

Red hesitated for a few more seconds. Then she slowly began padding into the unknown woods.

CHAPTER 16
EMI

EMI WALKED FOR hours, following Max's footprints past stubby pines and alder thickets, through brambles that clawed at her jeans and left tiny lacerations across her fists. Sometimes she thought she had lost his trail, and a bolt of terror would rise in her throat, but then she would see a pawprint, four round dots in front of a soft triangle, and her heart would settle back to normal.

If this had been the first time that Max had fled, Emi knew she would have felt very different from what she was experiencing now. She wasn't angry at him. And she wasn't angry at herself.

Instead, she was scared for Max. But she channeled that fear into action. She called for him until she was hoarse. She had followed his prints before; she knew how to follow them now.

She couldn't think at all about fleeing from her foster

home, from Jim and Meili and the baby. All she had room to worry about was Max and getting him back.

She walked until finally she came to the edge of a river with eroded banks, her boots squelching in the soft spring mud. It wasn't easy to keep her footing along the river's edge, but she managed, balancing her every step as downed trees forced her to clamber over their thick trunks. Glistening leaves fallen from the previous autumn hid deceptively deep pockets of water, and more than once the water came an inch from spilling over the top of her boots.

Emi wished she had brought more than one extra pair of socks. It had been at least ten degrees warmer at Jim and Meili's, with the cleared-out yard where sun warmed the ground and the air around it. Here, deep in the woods, her clothes seemed a feeble defense against the cold.

She was getting hungry, too. She tried to ignore it for the first couple of hours, but finally, when her belly howled so loudly she could hear it over the river, she stopped for a snack. She sat down next to a burly oak and leaned her back against the rough, dry bark. She opened her pack and took out her peanut butter and jelly sandwich.

Meili had showed her how to make it. First the peanut butter, then the jam, use two knives so you don't mix the two containers, make sure the tops line up, press lightly, then pack for later. Meili used the good kind of plastic bags, the ones that actually zipped closed instead of the folded-over-always-going-to-fail ones that Emi had usually used.

Emi felt an unexpected stab of loss. She hadn't meant to remember how excited she had felt when she had made her first sandwich. Her other foster parents never let her prepare anything for herself. Meili had trusted her to wield the two butter knives, to risk the mess on the kitchen counter-top. Emi had made her own meal from scratch and had been proud of it.

The last piece of sandwich stuck in her throat. She swallowed it, packed up, and continued on her way.

The dirt banks of the river gradually gave way to steep ledges. They had risen thirty feet above the winding water when Emi saw a flash of fur on the other side of the river.

"Max!" she screamed.

Max turned his head, his face a mask of joy as he saw Emi on the far embankment. He ran to the edge of his side of the river, paws scraping at the dirt, trying to find purchase, but the angle was too steep. He stared across at Emi, growling in frustration as he tried to find a way down.

"Hold on, Max, I'm coming!" Emi called.

Below her, the river raged, wide and foamy. Emi began to clamber down the steep side of the embankment, grabbing at slick roots poking out from the dirt to keep herself from falling. She was halfway down when the tree root she had been grasping to pull herself up slipped out of her hands like butter. Her other hand struck the dirt as she tried to steady herself, but a clod of wet clay came off and she was falling backward.

She hit the water hard. From below, a vicious current tugged at her body.

"No!" she screamed, water filling her mouth as she tumbled in the foaming river.

Emi struggled against the dark spring floodwater. She forced her arms to pull the water and arched her body upward. Her head broke the surface, and she gasped once, filling her lungs with sweet air, before the current took her down again.

The river was a devouring beast that was swallowing her whole. She fought it, but the relentless moving water tumbled her over and over until she was dizzy and icy, unsure of what way was up. Her backpack grew heavy as it filled with water, dragging her down.

Emi saw a glint of light and clawed her way toward it.

Her arms thrashed about, silently and desperately working her toward the surface, when suddenly she noticed how clear the water was. How delicately the sun seemed to glimmer through it. Everything was achingly serene. A sense of peace overcame her, sure and comforting, whole and true. She was okay. She was slipping into numbed happiness.

But there was one detail she could not forget. The part of her brain that was made of sheer survival was telling her something. She was not panicking, but some urgent, powerful voice inside her head was telling her to look up and see.

She stared at the ripples above her, wondering hazily why everything was so beautiful and strange and wrong. Then it occurred to her. She could see the surface of the water. Which meant that she was under the water. Which meant that she could not breathe. Which meant that she was drowning.

Shaking her head slowly side to side, Emi fought off the peaceful bliss that was filling her head and her lungs. She surged upward, her hands finding a strange power to propel her toward the sparkling light above her.

And then her head broke the surface, and she spat out the water in her lungs, half reviving, half choking as she treaded water in the wide, deep river. She heard a roaring in front of her, and she knew that she had to get out or she would be swept over the waterfall.

She struck out with her arms and started to swim toward upriver and toward the shore. Her boots and pack tugged her down, but she ignored them. She fought the river, screaming at it with her mind as she drew closer to the river's edge. She did not look back to see how close she was to the falls.

Stroke after stroke, Emi fought the river until her legs stumbled against the pebbled bottom. She staggered upright, pulling herself out of the river. Only then did she turn around.

The rush of pummeling water was deafening. She had come just ten feet from going over the waterfall.

And she was still on the same side of the river. After nearly drowning, she was no closer to Max than before.

Shivering, Emi crawled up the embankment. Only when she was safely away from its edge did she collapse onto the ground. Her fingers clutched the sweet, soft dirt. She was alive. She had survived. She could taste the tang of the wind in her mouth and feel the fibers of the tree roots that threaded around her.

The late-afternoon sun descended on her, and for a moment she felt utterly connected to the ground and the forest. As she drew in blissful gulps of air, the wildness of the place flooded through her lungs and down into her heart. It was as if tendrils of belonging had woven up through the ground, charged through the water soaking her skin, reshaping the blood in her body.

A cloud skated across the sky, and the setting sun winked out for a moment. Cold sliced through her reverie and filled her bones, making her shake. Emi shook her head and pulled herself to her feet.

"Max!" she screamed, hoping he could hear her from the other side of the river. "Max!"

There was no answer.

Night was coming, she was soaked with no dry clothes, and if she didn't find shelter soon, she was going to be in an awful lot of trouble.

And Max was still out there, lost. Emi's stomach curled into an ugly knot. What if Max had tried to follow her? What if he had tried to cross the river and had gone over the edge of the waterfall?

Emi rushed to the edge of the river and peered over the falls. Her eyes scanned the riverbanks below. She saw nothing. "Max!" she yelled again. Her only response was the howling of the water.

Another spasm of cold shook her, bringing her back to her immediate situation. She grabbed on to a slippery tree root and began to lower herself down the side of the waterfall. Clutching at rocks and branches, she half lowered, half slid down to where the falls ended in a pummeling roar of water.

She began to walk along the river, stumbling as the cold sank more deeply into her bones. She could feel a creeping numbness in her brain, making it hard to judge where to put her feet. She couldn't feel her fingers or her toes anymore. It became harder and harder to walk.

The sun disappeared, and the woods grew purple with twilight. Emi had trouble keeping her eyes open.

Just when she thought she could go no farther, she saw a shape in the distance. She rubbed her eyes to make sure she wasn't dreaming and looked again.

It was an old hunting cabin. Emi could see grime-covered windows and its sagging door. It was half-buried in weeds that crept along the sides of its mossy, rough-hewn log walls.

The door sat on hinges caked in rust. Emi tugged at the birch-branch door handle. The door inched open, protesting the entire way.

It was just as cold inside the shack as out, but there was no wind. There was a simple cot with a neatly folded wool blanket at the end of it. A tiny woodstove was tucked in the corner, along with a few pieces of ancient firewood stacked against the wall. Emi found a book of matches on a shelf next to the stove.

A small cry of relief lifted out of her throat. Everything had gone so horribly wrong that day, but to find shelter and warmth in the middle of a woods that had seemed so unforgiving felt like a much-needed miracle. One she had no business to expect would happen but was grateful for.

She silently thanked Jim for showing her how to start a fire as she quickly coaxed a few flames to life with her shaking hands. By the time the fire filled the stove, Emi had wrapped herself in the blanket. As she slowly warmed, she took stock of her bag. Her box of matches had turned into a wet, unusable mess, and she was filled with gratitude toward whoever had left the matches in the cabin. Some of her food had survived being dumped into the river, and Max's bag of doggie treats still remained, but she had lost his entire bag of kibble, and most of her sandwiches had been turned into soggy mush.

On top of all that, her clothes were completely soaked.

She draped her socks, shirts, and underwear on the floor next to the stove and then huddled there herself, watching thin steam rise from her drying clothes.

It was a few hours before she was truly warm, and even longer before she allowed herself to sink into the bed.

She lay awake, thinking about Max and how much she wished he was at her feet, warming her toes, until her exhausted eyelids drooped and she fell into a dreamless, exhaustion-heavy slumber.

CHAPTER 17
MAX

Max's Guide to Falling in Love

1. Set the mood. There should be a river. Maybe some sticks. Afternoon light.

2. Be in the middle of howling your head off.

3. Mid howl, see the girl.

4. See the girl see you.

5. Feel a single point of joy so powerful, you forget to breathe.

6. Everything disappears. River. Sticks. Light. Gone.

There is just you and the girl, staring at each other, as if everything in the whole world has melted away and the two of you are all there is.

7. Run to the girl. Get stopped by the river. Stupid river is real, after all.

8. Realize just how much you love the girl when the girl begins to come to you and suddenly plunges into the river.

Max felt the breath flood out of him. His head grew dizzy. He wanted desperately to leap out and grab the girl, drag her to safety from the clutches of the river—but his paws felt like they were encased in concrete.

Time tumbled about him slowly—he could see the crust of the river's edge giving way, the tiny root hairs that came off in the girl's hand as she fell, the flow of her hair as it swirled around her face, the crumbling sound of rock and dirt sliding downhill, and the slap of the water as she hit it. He saw her disappear into the churning water, the waves frothing about her body.

When she reappeared farther down the river, Max

snapped out of his trance, forcing his frozen legs to move downriver. He galloped along the riverbank, barking and whining, willing the girl to return to him, to climb back up the bank and keep him safe.

Instead, in the dying evening light, he saw her drag herself out of the water and collapse on the other side of the river. Max could hear the deafening cascade of a waterfall just beyond. There was no way he could reach the girl. He was stuck on the wrong side, alone in the woods.

Max's tail wilted. He barked and barked until he was hoarse. On the other side, he could see her yelling for him. But neither could hear the other over the roar of the water.

Look at me, girl! Look! Max howled. *See me and know that I'm trying to get to you!*

It was no use, though. No matter how much he woofed and ran back and forth and tried to make a visible spectacle of himself, the girl did not turn his way. He watched as she pulled herself up onto the far bank and disappeared into the woods.

Max darted frantically back up the river, scouting for a place where he could cross. He spotted a shallow dip in the embankment and scrambled down it. But when he tried to wade into the water, the pull of the current made him draw back. He was no match for the ferocity of the water.

Max clambered up the embankment and sat. He would just have to figure something else out. Max had no doubt he would find his way out of this pickle. Maybe he would . . . just . . . stay in place?

No. He wouldn't find the girl that way.

Think, Max, think, he thought to himself.

He had it! The river was like his tail—wide in some parts, skinny in others, wagging from side to side sometimes, too. He had been thinking that he should cross at a skinny part. But the water flowed so deeply and quickly there, he couldn't battle it.

He just needed to find the opposite of skinny. If skinny was deep, wide might be shallow.

Once he found a wide part, he would cross, find the girl on the other side, they would all go home, and he would get kibble.

Max began to walk along the edge of the river. It was starting to get late, but he kept his eyes trained on the far shore, looking for a place where it stretched out instead of hugged close to his side.

He was going along, minding his own business when, in the distance, there was a howl in the night.

The patch of fur above Max's tail flicked straight up. He scanned the area. Another howl echoed along the trees, this time from a different direction.

Hey, I think those are my coyote cousins! Max thought. *Great! I can ask them for directions.*

But then he remembered something. Or rather, he heard something. It was Red's voice. In his head, warning him.

They eat everything.

Everything.

When he heard another howl, low and calculating, Max began to run. His heart skittered as he felt the blood pulsing through his legs. Everything came into sharp detail. He could see each individual new spring leaf on each tree, the way that droplets of water glinted off their edges. He saw the grooved patterns in old oak trunks, the ants and grubs crawling about them as they scavenged for food. He dodged a fallen log and plunged through a bramble bush, wincing as the small thorns raked across his sides.

He wasn't fast enough. His big paws kept tripping over too many roots and twigs, and once, his back leg tripped his front leg, catapulting him straight into the ground. He could hear the coyotes around him now, running to catch up, working to flank him.

Max fled across the forest, the wind whipping his scratched and bleeding coat. He glanced around him. There were five coyotes chasing him, two on either side, and one behind him. They were smaller than he was, but fast.

He was panting so hard he could hardly breathe, but he still had enough in his lungs to let out a tiny, scared whimper. As he did, he caught a flash of sunset-colored fur ahead of him. He blinked once, just to make sure he wasn't imagining things.

"Come with me," said Red. "Right. Now." She began to lope through the woods in short, blisteringly fast spurts.

Max looked back at the coyotes. The nearest one lifted its upper lips. Max could see the saliva dripping off its fangs. As the coyotes sprang toward him again, Max turned his back and galloped after Red. He followed her away from the river, through the trees, and to the front of a dirt hole dug out of the side of a hill. Tufts of long brown winter-dead grass hung over the entrance.

"Max, let's go!" Red snapped. She turned and disappeared into the hole.

When he reached the entrance of the dirt cave, Max hurled himself inside. He searched for a second entrance to wriggle out and found none.

They were trapped. Red had led him into a trap!

"Relax, Max," said Red.

"There's no way out!" barked Max. "We're coyote meat for sure!"

Red lifted her nose. "No. We're not."

"But . . ."

"Max," said Red patiently, "please, just wait."

Max turned toward the opening. He could feel blood sliding down his sides. He could just imagine how the smell of it was whetting the appetites of the coyotes. He felt the walls of the cave rise around him, closing him in, surrounding him with the scent of his own fear. Every muscle tensed as he readied himself for one last explosive run through the gauntlet of coyote teeth and claws.

He waited. But the coyotes did not come. He could hear them pacing around the cave, but they did not venture inside. And a few minutes later, he heard the sound of fading footsteps. And then, nothing.

Confused, Max cautiously poked his nose outside. He saw no sign of the coyote pack that had been so eager to eat him. He returned to Red. Somehow, Red had found the only place where they were safe.

Red went up to Max and nuzzled his throat, purring. "Come on," she said. "We've got to go."

Max looked around the cave. It was warm and dry. He could see the light fading through the drooping blades of grass. It would be night soon. "Why don't we stay here tonight?" he asked.

"Max, why do you think the coyotes didn't follow us inside?" Red asked.

Max shrugged. "Because they were scared?"

"And why would they be scared?" Red asked. "Look around you, Max. Sniff the air. Tell me what you think."

Max lifted his nose and took a breath. The air was warm and musty, with a strong odor of fat and fur. "Someone lives here," he said. "Someone big."

"It's a bear den," said Red. "And when it comes back, it isn't going to be happy about two animals spending the night in its home."

"So what should we do?" Max asked.

Red paused, one foot lifted as she headed toward the entrance. "We can't stay here—this place isn't safe for us, either." She brought her foot down lightly. "We are going to leave this den, find a safe place to hide for the night, and in the morning we are going to go straight home."

"No," said Max.

Red's tail lashed in the dimming light. "What do you mean no?"

Max got to his feet. "I'll leave, but I'm not going to look for a place to sleep. I've got to get the girl."

Red glided to Max. She sat precisely in front of him, staring at him from inches away. "Max. How many times do I have to tell you? You don't know how to survive out in the woods. You almost got eaten by coyotes today. You don't know where that girl is going or where she might end up. And I don't know this area of the woods well. I can't tell you what animals are out there or how dangerous they are. If you go after the girl, there is a very good chance that you are going to die. You can't protect yourself. And I can't protect you.

"Plus," she added, "did it ever occur to you that you would be more helpful going back to the man and the woman and yowling your head off so they search for her themselves instead of us going out on our own?"

"I didn't think of that," said Max.

"That's why you've nearly gotten killed every time you've

stepped outside!" snapped Red. "You have to think when you're outside. *All the time.* And not just about what you want to do, but what you need to do. Not every answer is easy in the woods. And right now, I'm telling you that the answer is to let the girl go. She can find her way back home by herself—you being around her will probably only get her into trouble because you'll get yourself into trouble and she'll have to save you. Think, for once, Max. Think, and come home with me. I know the way."

Max stiffened. "I know you make sense, Red, but I left the girl on the other side of the river. She is cold and alone. She fell into the water, and I didn't go after her. I was too scared. But I'm not going back until we find her. She's my person and I lo—"

"Max, watch out!" Red leaped past Max. Confused, he turned and saw a shaggy, lumbering body filling the space where the cave entrance used to be.

"Uh-oh," he said.

Red ran straight toward the bear and catapulted onto its head, aiming her piercing claws at its eyes. As the bear lifted a huge paw, Red met Max's eyes.

"Run, Max. Run," she said.

Max barked. The bear roared and charged at him, with

Red still on its face. It was so much bigger than any of the coyotes. One bite from the bear, and he would be gone.

Ducking under the bear's legs, Max followed Red's orders and scrambled out of the den, then bolted tail-down into the night.

CHAPTER 18
RED

RED KNEW SHE couldn't fight the bear on her own. She jumped off its head as it swatted at her and backed away, hissing and spitting. The bear filled the entire entrance, snorting as it charged her.

Red retreated to the corner of the den. She could feel the dirt crumbling into her fur as she pressed against the den wall. The bear padded toward her. In the dull dusk light, she could see its wet black nose, the cruel intelligence of its eyes as it stalked her. The bear opened its mouth, exposing a pair of yellowed incisors. She was more than just an intruder in its space—she was a potential meal.

Out of the corner of her eye, Red spotted a glint of fading light. It was coming from a small hole in the ceiling of the den, a burrow from when a smaller animal used to inhabit the space. As the bear lunged, she sprang toward the opening.

Red felt a whiff of hot breath as its jaws clamped down on the end of her tail. A tuft of fur gave way as she ripped herself free from the bear's jaws. She wriggled through the burrow, inching upward until she could smell the cold, fresh spring air outside.

She could also smell the musk of coyotes drifting in the wind. The sun had long set, and even the purple dusk was fading into the darkness of night.

Red hesitated. She could hear the muffled shuffling of the bear as it turned about its den. She was still so close she could smell its thick fur, but she didn't think the bear would destroy its own den in order to dig her out from the tunnel.

She found a level part of the burrow and curled up in a ball. She was safe here—the burrow smelled of rich soil and old animal scent. No one had used it in a while.

Red tucked her nose into the soft, thick fluff of her belly. She would stay there until morning. Then she would find Max and drag his foolish, furry body back to the safety of the house.

As she lay there in the cold, she thought about why she was risking her life for the sake of Max. He should mean nothing to her. The girl shouldn't, either.

And yet. Red frowned, confused. Her whole life was a

set of precise calculations, designed for hunting prey and keeping alive. She had no use for anyone. But here she was, protecting a dog—of all animals—and realizing, with a flicker of surprise, that she was worried about him.

Maybe she was getting old. Maybe there was part of her that was still calculating, judging the power of her jaws and legs to be weaker than they were a year ago, two years ago, and her brain was leading her toward companionship so that she would be taken care of as she aged.

That must be it, Red thought, satisfied. *A practical reason for why I'm doing all of this. Because it wouldn't make sense that I, a cat, would be growing fond of a dog.*

That couldn't be it at all, she thought as she drifted to sleep.

She woke to thick rain falling above her. She could hear it scatter across the new spring leaves and drip into a little puddle on the ground. It crept into the edges of the burrow but didn't reach her sleeping spot. Red had intended to head out at first light, but the rain did not let up until well into the afternoon.

When the sound of raindrops finally dimmed to an occasional drip, Red crawled to the entrance of the tunnel. She looked around to make sure the bear or coyotes weren't lying in wait. When she saw nothing, she pulled herself outside and stretched.

The bear den was dug out of a small hill dotted with maple trees. Red remembered that she had run upward to find it and began to pad down the hill. As she walked, she searched for dog tracks in the wet mud.

She found them a hundred yards away, distinct impressions followed by slick scrapes in the mud as they clambered up a steep gully. She saw claw lines raked across a wall of dirt, and a second set of tracks leading up and over the gully.

Max had been here. He had slipped and slid down the gully and run up it again. Red sniffed the ground. Coyotes had been here, too. They had hunted Max. She smelled traces of blood. She didn't know if it was dog or coyote.

At the top of the gully, the pawprints ended at the edge of a smooth, grassy field. Red looked around. She saw a small ledge jutting out from the mountain. Trotting past a fallen log, she went to the ledge and looked out. Below her, she could see the thread of river that had led her into the woods and the waterfall spilling out a mile away.

Max's trail had gone cold. Red stopped to think. If he had made it to where she was, perhaps he had spotted the waterfall and remembered that it was where the girl had fallen. If so, that's where he would be headed.

Red pointed her nose in the direction of the falls and began to make her way down the mountain. It was new terrain, so she concentrated all her attention on keeping her direction pointed firmly toward her destination.

Behind her, something followed.

CHAPTER 19
EMI

EMI AWOKE TO the thumping of rain on the roof. She shivered, clutching the wool blanket to her chest to soak in a few more minutes of warmth. When she finally rose, she kept the blanket draped around her shoulders as she shuffled out of the cot.

She went to the window and stared out of it, willing Max to appear. She hoped that if she wanted it hard enough, he would suddenly come bounding out of the woods and to the door.

But the pane of glass showed nothing but fat raindrops and glistening trees. Emi sat and thought, tapping her finger to her mouth. She knew if she went searching for Max, it would take a miracle to find him. There were no trails to follow, and searching for signs of him would be like trying to find a grain of salt in a bowl of sugar. She could retrace her steps and go to where she had tumbled down the embankment, but she knew that Max wouldn't have stayed there long. He could be anywhere in the woods by now.

The morning rain faded, and glints of afternoon sun peeked through. It was time to leave the cabin and find Max. Emi looked around. She decided to take the blanket with her—even though it wasn't winter anymore, she had been surprised at how cold it had gotten during the night. If she wasn't going to make it back to the cabin tonight, she wanted to be prepared.

She hunted around and took a few more items—the book of matches; a handful of kindling in case she couldn't find any dry, dead wood; a few newspapers; and all the food on the shelf—packets of sugar and salt, a tin of sardines, and a small box of crackers. She could use all the food she could find.

She repacked her bag, found some twine, and strapped the blanket to the outside of it. Then she hitched her supplies onto her shoulders, twisted her bracelet, and headed out the door to find her dog.

A patch of sunlight had broken through the trees. Emi stepped into it and raised her face to the sky. She closed her eyes and soaked in the warmth, feeling it trail down her entire body. She ripped open a sugar packet and tipped the contents into her mouth. Then, with a jolt of energy flooding through her, she turned away from the river, went to the back of the shack, and staring straight ahead, she began to walk.

A few seconds later, she walked straight into a briar patch. Stinging prickers pierced through her pants and yanked against her jacket. She stopped, muttering to herself as she pulled out loose thorns that had embedded themselves into her socks.

When she was done, she continued on her way. She walked until the brush split open and gave way to a boulder field that filled up the side of a mountain.

Emi peered up. Near the top of the mountain, she could see a ledge jutting out like a great stone nose. Her heart lifted. She bet there was a good view up there. One where she could see the whole of the valley, and maybe even a dog that she was desperate to find.

And if she didn't see Max, she was also willing to bet that if she yelled there, he would hear her. There would be no river roar to drown out her calling to him.

She shifted the pack on her shoulders and began to pick her way across the unsteady ground. She tested each boulder with a cautious foot before putting her full weight on it, but a few still wobbled when she pushed off them.

She was halfway up the field when she heard a deep rumbling. She looked up. The mountain was sliding down, heading straight for her.

Emi began to run. The very rocks that she had judged so carefully going up she skittered across recklessly, her shoes barely touching the wobbly stone. She could hear the snaky hiss of sand shifting and the clatter of pebbles, followed by the sharp, hollow cracks of large boulders tumbling down the mountain. All the sounds were catching up to her.

Her world focused into the shapes of the rocks in front of her. She didn't have time to see the future—she could see only the next step and hope that she was going in the right direction. She judged each angle without thinking, her feet skipping desperately over the rocks as she raced the oncoming avalanche. Pebbles hit the backs of her legs, and she knew the boulders were coming next.

She whipped her head around. She could see the boulders fifty feet above her, rushing down with impartial fury. There was no time to outrun the avalanche. In just moments, she would be crushed.

To her right, Emi saw a shadow. A hump of rock jutted

out over the steep ground, the space underneath it an inky unknown. With the roaring of the boulders in her ears, Emi pivoted and lunged toward the rock. Her shoulder slammed painfully into the ground, but she slid into the crevice just as the first of the boulders came.

The sound was terrifying. Emi huddled against the cold, damp stone, covering her ears with the palms of her hands. Her throat burst open into a scream, but she couldn't hear her voice over the thundering of the rock.

As the mountain fell around her, Emi felt her rock shelter shudder but hold.

When the boulders finally started to slow, she uncovered her ears and realized with surprise that she was still scream-ing. She could hear herself a little now. But she was okay. She was okay!

She would beat this avalanche. She would survive, and she would go on; she would find Max, and she would bring him home. When the boulders finally stopped falling, Emi stepped out from the overhang and hollered her triumph to the world. She threw up her hands and leaped, her body a defiant arch against gravity.

As she came down, the tip of her right shoe slid into a crack between two rocks. When she tried to pull it out, the mess of rocks under her feet shifted. Emi fell flat on her back, her knees bent to the sky, her pack pulling her helplessly down as though she were an upturned turtle.

Her arms flew over her head and she heard a sharp crack.

No, Emi thought. *No, please no, please.*

But when she looked up and to her left, she saw them. Two broken pieces of jade, part of a circle that would never be whole again.

"Mom!" Emi screamed. The only thing that she had left from her life with her mother was gone. Broken. By her. She closed her eyes and felt herself sliding back into that last day they had spent together.

They had been in a hospital, surrounded by bags of clear fluid hanging from metal poles and the smell of cleaning chemicals. Her mom was hooked up to a beeping machine and holding Emi's hand as lightly as a songbird's breath, but whenever Emi had squeezed it, she had squeezed right back.

Until she didn't.

That was the moment when the cancer that had spread through her liver with ferocious speed finally took her. Powerful, ugly, cruel mutant cells had cut down the strongest, most beautiful woman in the world.

Emi closed her hands around the broken stone bracelet and cupped them to her chest. Then she lay there for a long time, eyes closed, tears slipping down as freely as rain.

Then, when she was done, she wiped her eyes, tucked the pieces in her pocket, unclipped the straps of her pack, and sat up. She would always carry the ache of that memory in her heart. And she would honor it and allow herself to grieve for as long as she needed.

But right now, she had some surviving to do. She grasped her stuck leg with both hands and tugged to free herself.

Her foot would not budge.

CHAPTER 20
MAX

Max's Guide to Falling in Love . . . Again

1. Wake up to rain dripping on your nose.

2. Sniff at the rotten leaves surrounding you.

3. Uncurl your body and stretch.

4. Begin to yawn.

5. *Wait a minute.*

6. Red.

7. RED?

8. RED!!!!!

9. WHY DID YOU LEAVE RED BEHIND WITH A BEAR?!

10. Well, okay, she told you to go, and she knows best. But still, maybe you should have done something to help her. Even if it meant fighting a bear.

11. Think about what it meant for Red to let you go and save yourself. To face a danger she may not have survived. For you. To save you.

12. Feel that same tug in your heart as when you fell for the girl.

13. THE GIRL.

14. FIND THE GIRL.

15. Find Red?

16. You love the girl. You love Red.

17. WHAT DO YOU DOOOOOO?

As Max struggled out from underneath the log, it occurred to him that freedom was very different from what he had thought. When he was in the shelter, he had dreamed intensely of cageless skies and limitless fields in which to pee and frolic.

Now here he was, as free as his dream, but instead of feeling liberated, he felt worried. He could do anything, but he didn't know what to do or where to go.

He unloaded his bladder on a tree, and then he trotted one way and then the other, trying to figure out if it was the girl he should follow, or Red.

Then he realized that it didn't matter. He didn't know how to find either of them.

He began to whine, then stopped. Being nervous wouldn't help anything. He had to think. He had to make a plan.

Start retracing your steps. Go back to the bear den and see if Red is there. If she isn't, get to the river. That's where you last saw the girl, and where she might still be. This way, you can be looking for both the girl and Red. You don't have to decide between the two of them—hooray!

Max shook the water out of his fur and got to hunting.

His nose sniffed out the faint track of where he had been before. He knew that if he followed the scent of himself, he would be able to retrace his steps back to the bear den. Lowering his head, Max got to work.

His feet padded through the mud as he inhaled. The rain made all the smells come to life. He could smell the winter trails of mice and voles, soft hints of underground chipmunk burrows, rotting leaves, awakening ticks and flies.

A pile of poop made him pause. He could smell bone fragments and see splotches of fur in it. Coyotes.

Max whipped his head up. He searched the trees for a sign of the coyote pack. When he didn't see anything, he bent his head to the pile of dung and sniffed again. His heart stopped hammering. The scent was fading. Whenever the coyote had stopped, it had not been recently.

A different smell brought Max's head back to the ground again. He sniffed harder, just to make sure.

He was sure. It was Red's scent, a feline mix of predator and fur.

Max's ears perked up. A clue! Red wasn't at the bear den—she was here! Or, close to here.

New plan! He could find Red, and then she would know how to get them all out of this mess.

Of course. He shook his head, surprised he hadn't thought of it before when he decided who to go after. He had Red's scent—he could follow it to her and give his freedom over to her, deferring to the wisdom of her years in the woods. He wouldn't have to make a decision only to realize that it was a dumb mistake, over and over again.

He bent his head to Red's smell and followed it until he heard the familiar sound of crashing water in the distance. Jerking his head up, he raced through the trees until he came across the cliff where he had seen the girl disappear.

He knew where he was—finally! This place was the closest clue he had to finding the girl, and he needed to use it.

New new plan—get the girl! Max growled. Freedom was hard. It felt like a lot of thinking.

Above the foaming spray, he saw the place where he had seen the girl crawl out of the water, and even though he knew that crossing the river was dangerous and almost certainly another dumb mistake, and that Red was on his side of the river and not the girl's, Max ran upriver, wading through thickets of low grass and brush, until he spotted a few tall boulders sticking out of the water like thumbs.

The current was wicked here, the water swelling up the

banks. The river had been fed by the rain from the previous night, and it was angry.

Max didn't care. He had changed his mind too many times in the past hour, and he was going to stick with the plan he had. He charged toward the river, and as his front paws splashed into the water, he made a mighty leap and landed on the first boulder.

The rock was slippery with algae and moss. Max's claws scrabbled against it, the sheer force of his determination propelling him up to the top of the boulder. Once he was there, he kept going.

Hop. Scrabble. Hop. Scrabble. Hop. Whoops.

Max belly flopped into the river. The current yanked at him, pulling him away from the boulder he had been aiming for.

Max opened his mouth to whine, and water flooded in. He snorted and shook his head. *No time to whine, mister*, he told himself. *Time to survive.*

He concentrated his energy into his legs, feeling them work by some ancient instinct as they churned through the water, keeping him afloat. He pointed his nose in the direction of the opposite shore and started paddling hard. Every other thought left him. He was Max, dog swimmer, girl/cat steadfast friend, survivor.

His feet touched bottom. With a few wobbly stumbles forward, Max pulled himself out of the river. He had made it. His fur was soaked, and his claws had been grated shorter. But he was on the same side as the girl.

Max let out a happy, excited yip and got to work. He trotted downriver, then lowered his head to the dirt and began to sniff. There it was—coconut and lemon. He shook his tail so hard, he nearly fell over.

He would find the girl, and she would find Red, and they would all go home, and he would never have to make a plan again!

CHAPTER 21
RED

RED STOOD IN front of the waterfall, watching the foamy spray tumble down into the blank river below. Step by step, she had found her way there. But Max had not; neither had the girl. She had searched a mile up and down the river for them and come up with nothing. Her plan to find them had failed.

Red stopped, checking herself. She had been so intent on getting back to the waterfall, now that she was there and did not have to concentrate on navigating, the rest of her body came into focus. A surge of hunger rushed to the surface, clamoring for attention. She had not eaten for two days. She had to hunt.

Red turned from the river and made her way into the forest. She came to a fallen rotted oak, its roots tipped in the air, mossy bark peeling off its decaying trunk.

Red crawled into the damp space between the tree and the ground and lay hidden in the darkness. Her eyes scanned the forest floor. She waited.

Robins and blue jays sang overhead, far out of reach. A toad hopped across the dirt, its dry, bumpy back nearly invisible against the old leaves. A rustle of wind blew across the old ruin of log and passed.

In the quiet of the dying wind, Red saw a flicker of movement. She crouched, her muscles rigid as she held herself back. There was a chipmunk crawling down a nearby maple tree, its puffy little tail whipping back and forth. It hopped to the ground and stood upright, its paws curled up under its nose. Its whiskers quivered as it sniffed the air.

Red deepened into her crouch. She loved this moment—the stillness before the pounce.

The chipmunk bounded closer to the fallen log, its juicy little body hopping closer and closer to Red. Suddenly, it dived into the leaves and disappeared.

Red waited. She heard nails shuffling away tiny mounds of dirt. A few minutes later, the chipmunk emerged, an acorn stuffed into the pocket of one of its cheeks.

In one smooth leap, Red burst out from the darkness and launched herself at her prey. As she came down, the chipmunk squeaked and jumped forward. Red's paws landed on the chipmunk's tail.

As she bent her mouth over the chipmunk, it spat the acorn out of its mouth and pulled free. Red pounced again, but the chipmunk sprang in the opposite direction she was expecting, and she had to reverse her body mid leap. She twisted toward her breakfast. Her teeth clipped a tuft of fur that slid out of her mouth.

Before Red could leap again, the chipmunk had hurled itself at the base of the striped maple tree. Red pulled out her claws and shimmied up the base, but the smooth bark slid out against her and she fell back down to the ground. Above her, the chipmunk chittered an angry warning.

Red glared at the chipmunk. Every prey in the area would know her presence now. She would just have to hunt elsewhere.

CHAPTER 22
MAX

Max's Guide to Understanding What He Really Wants, Now That He's Had a Taste of Freedom

1. Well, it's obvious that you want to be with the girl. That's why you're tracking her. Duh.

2. Speaking of tracking her . . . you've lost her scent. Nuts.

3. Race around in circles, sniffing, snorting, confusing yourself. You've got to find her smell, or you're never going to get treats again!

4. Treats. You also really want treats.

5. But it's something more. Something deeper.

6. You stop, mid track, thinking.

7. It's not just the girl and the treats that you want. You want them at the house, surrounded by the walls that keep the wind at bay, next to the backyard that's full of your wonderful pee scent. You want them in a familiar place.

8. You want the girl and treats. And you want them at home.

Max didn't want to be free in the woods anymore. Running around by himself for just one day had cured him of the absolute ability he had to be wherever he wanted. He missed the dirt road that led up to the house, the warmth of the inside of the house. He missed hogging the best spot by the fireplace, with dinnertime always a given.

Most of all, he missed the girl. There was a pull in his gut, deeper than the hunger that gnawed at his insides, that he didn't quite fully understand but knew was part of him. It was as if he felt like a thin leash linked the two of them, and the farther they got from each other, the more likely it would snap.

If it snapped, Max didn't know what he would do.

Right now, though, he had to concentrate. He bent his nose to the ground. Two months ago, he would have tried to figure out every single smell that hit his nose. But today was different. Now he was hunting for a very specific smell. It was of lemon soap and wet human hair.

His nostrils flickered as he inhaled in short, sharp breaths. He could smell rotten leaves. Mouse poop. New grass and dying grass. The acrid scent of ant trails. Squirrel pee.

Squirrel!

Max automatically looked up, scanning the ground. There, ahead of him, a squirrel sat on a mossy rock, bending its head toward its paws, which were holding an acorn.

Max's mouth began to water. He took a step toward the squirrel. The squirrel, completely absorbed in its breakfast, didn't flinch. He took another step, and another. He could get it . . . he knew he could.

And then, wafting across his nose, there came the slightest trace of something familiar.

It was the smell of wool and jeans and citrus. It was the girl. The scent was so delicate, Max knew he would lose it if the wind picked up.

Without having to think, Max abandoned the squirrel

and trained his nose toward the girl's smell. He kept sniffing, walking slowly, carefully, tracing her trail. The world dissolved around him. There was nothing but sniffs and snorts and the slow, long hunt for the girl who he loved.

As he buried his nose in his work, Max did not hear the soft crackle of leaves behind him. He did not see the hunched, slinking animal slowly closing in on him. It was only when he caught the wild smell of fur that he looked up to see the shape of a fully grown coyote only a few paces away.

Max froze. The coyote was straight in front of him. Its yellow eyes were focused and cold. He saw the hind muscles bunch up.

Max whirled and leaped sideways. As he did, he saw the female coyote rushing toward him, a blur of steel-colored power. He skidded short, his paws digging into the mud. His tail flattened out into a frantic line as he began to run, and both coyotes gave chase.

Max felt the heat rising in his body as he fled his hunters. There was no room to remember his hunger, or his search. He ran with the grim knowledge that if he stopped, he would not stay alive. And he knew that wherever he could go, so could the coyotes. He didn't have Red to show him where to hide or how to be safe.

The female coyote lunged up, and her teeth caught the edge of Max's ear. He felt the soft tissue tearing, and a needle-sharp pain dug into him. Yanking his head up, Max tore free from the coyote and leaped away. A slow drip of blood trickled down the side of his face.

The male coyote flanked him, running with easy, sure strides. As they reached the edge of the forest and emerged onto a boulder field, he struck Max in the shoulder.

Max flew into the air and landed hard on his back. As he twisted to find his footing, the male coyote clamped his jaws down on the soft underside of Max's neck.

Max drew one short breath before his windpipe flattened. The coyote's breath smelled delicious—a combination of rot and blood and meat. Max gasped for air as the coyote inched his jaws tighter into the scruff of his neck, getting closer to completely cutting off his ability to breathe.

Streaks of light began to zoom across Max's eyes. Suddenly, he felt like he was underwater, slipping into a fuzzy heaviness. As darkness began to creep across him, warm and gentle despite the face of the coyote attached to him, he heard a voice.

"Max! Max!"

Max shook his head weakly. His ears swiveled toward the familiar sound.

"Max!"

It was the girl. She was fifty feet away from him, lying at an unnatural angle in the boulder field. And she was screaming.

The darkness fled from Max's eyes, leaving him terribly, violently awake. He arched his back and bared every single one of his teeth. A deep-throated growl he didn't know he could make ripped out of him. It was low and vibrating and came from deep inside his throat.

His eyes dilated, and his mouth curled into a snarl. He struck out with his hind legs, his claws scoring the underside of the coyote's belly.

The coyote's grip on his neck loosened. Max lashed his forelegs out and curled them around the coyote's face. His scrabbling claws inched up the coyote's snout, and his teeth reached forward until they connected with the soft jelly of its eye.

The coyote spit out Max's scruff and backed off, brushing his eye with a hairy paw.

Max flipped onto his feet. He saw the female coyote lunging toward him from the side.

This time Max did not run away. He squared his

shoulders and faced the coyote, the back of his fur bristling. His lips curled, revealing yellowed teeth that rivaled the coyote's, Max rushed at her, his mouth open, his eyes two pinpricks of concentrated fury. He attacked her with bites and kicks and snarls, a tornado of wildness that seemed to come from the ancient depths of his soul. He would not be cornered. He would not be eaten. He would protect his girl.

The female backed away. Her tail dropped below her legs. She turned and began to run back into the forest.

Max leaped after her but stopped short when he reached the forest's edge. His focus had been on getting free from the predators, but there was something far more important to him in the opposite direction.

He circled back to where the male coyote had dropped to the ground, still pawing at his eyes. Max ran past him, through the boulder field, and up to the rocks, where he could see the most beautiful face he had ever known.

The explosion of her warm, familiar scent in his nostrils filled him with a raw joy that evaporated all the hurt and hunger of the morning. He wriggled, his tail thumping, trying to nose his way closer against his human.

But the girl did not embrace him as she normally did.

Instead, she stiffened and drew back as he approached her.

As he closed in on her, he saw a look on the girl's face. He had seen it only once before, but he recognized it immediately. It was the look the woman had given him before the man had taken him to the shelter. It was fear.

Fear of what he might do.

Max stopped. He was inches from the girl, a breath away from licking her cheeks and her hands and telling her he loved her, but when he leaned over to the girl, she pushed him away and shook her head.

"Go away!" she yelled. "No."

Max crouched and whimpered. He knew what that tone of voice meant. He was not wanted. He was not welcome.

He had worked so hard to find the girl. But he forced himself to back away and not beg for the welcoming hug he was looking forward to so badly.

CHAPTER 23
EMI

WHEN MAX APPEARED at the edge of the boulder field, Emi's heart leaped. He had found her! She opened her mouth, his name on her lips.

But then she saw him driving forward, his eyes a shade of cold fury she had never seen before. As he attacked the coyotes, the relief she had felt melted away, replaced by the words of the animal shelter worker.

Pit bulls. Reputation for being vicious.

When Max bit the coyote in the eye, Emi shrieked, the sound rising from her throat thick as nausea. She had never known the side of him that existed that could behave so ferociously.

Then, when Max had driven the coyotes off and come to Emi, she could see his eyes were calming down, but there was still a slash of that rage that lingered.

There was blood on his muzzle. Some of it wasn't his.

She yanked at her stubborn boot, willing it to spring free of the boulder. It did not budge, and as Max approached her, Emi was afraid. She let out a yell that drove him back, his paws tumbling over themselves in haste and confusion.

"Go away!" Emi screamed. "No!"

Max backed up, ears drooping, as though he were trying to shield himself from the force of her yell.

Emi sat, looking at Max silently, trying to understand what he had become to her in the space of what had felt like an endless coyote-fur-and-blood-biting moment. How could Max, her Max, have done such a thing? How would she know he wouldn't do it to her?

Max slid onto the ground, his head between his paws. A soft whine escaped his throat. He stretched forward, belly scraping across the ground, wanting to be with her but keeping his distance because he knew that was what she wanted.

The combination of longing and obedience broke Emi. It was just like how she felt in the foster home before Jim and Meili's, when she had thought those foster parents would have actually been the ones to adopt her. She had tried so hard to be the perfect kid—quiet, polite, studious, helpful—and had an almost promise of adoption papers being filled out on a hopeful Monday.

Then Tuesday had come with fifth-period social studies class, when Mr. Davis had been discussing different kinds of historical family structures—nuclear, single-parent, extended, stepfamilies, and everything in between. He had asked students to describe their perfect home family.

That's when Brad Dobbins had leaned over and whisper-sang in her ear, "Doesn't matter what kind of family you've got, it'll never be perfect because you're a reject orphan."

Emi had felt something deep down in her start to burn with rage, and before she knew it, she had thrown her weighty, 375-page history textbook at Brad, ended up in the principal's office, and two weeks later, she had gone straight back into the merry-go-round of the foster care system.

She had thrown the book out of hurt and rage, but it wasn't who she was. The act labeled her as trouble, and no matter what she did, she couldn't seem to escape that judgment.

She would not do that to Max. While attacking the coyotes, Max was trying to protect her. She would not define the entirety of his character based on one fierce moment.

"Max," Emi called, her voice quiet now, "come."

Max came to her, and she met him with her arms flung

wide, grabbing him before he had fully reached her and pulling him into a giant hug. "Max," she whispered. "My boy. My sweet boy. Thank you for finding me."

She opened her pack and pulled out the Ziploc bag of Milk-Bone treats. Max's nose was in her face as she opened the plastic packaging. She held out handfuls of treats for him to gobble up, allowing herself to laugh as his tongue warmed the palms of her hands.

When she was done feeding him, she tried again to free her leg from the tumbled rock. She clawed the rock behind her and tugged as hard as she could. Her foot was still stubbornly wedged between the two rocks.

Max danced around her, barking and yipping. He crouched and pounced at her, his paws batting at her arms. Emi grabbed his ears between her hands and wrestled him, kissing his dirty head as he pulled away. He ran at her again and seized her arm in his mouth. Emi felt his excitement overwhelm him as he clamped down on her.

"Okay, okay," she told Max. "Easy, there."

Max woofed and wiggled—his butt going side to side in a happy dance that made her laugh—and let go. He stood there, his tongue lolling about as he panted and drooled, his mouth stretched into the widest of grins.

Emi stroked his head softly. "I love you, too, buddy," she told him. She kissed him and wrapped her arms around his body as he snuggled close.

"Oh, Max," she said. "I've gotten myself into a mess, and I don't know how to get out of it. What am I going to do?"

Max woofed and licked her. Then he wriggled out of her arms and looked up at her with expectant eyes.

Emi laughed. "You have no idea what's going on, you just want to play. Okay, then." She looked around and saw a small stick nestled among the rocks. She picked it up and threw it, just like the way she threw Max's tug toy back home. "There you go," she said.

Max barked and leaped toward the stick. Clipping it between his teeth, he trotted back and proudly dropped it in front of her, his tail flipping around like a windshield wiper in a torrential rainstorm.

Emi picked it up and threw the stick again. It bounced off a rock and skittered out of sight. Max ran, barking, toward it and disappeared.

Emi waited. "Max?" she called. "What are you doing?"

Max emerged from the dip in the rock grunting. In his mouth was a stick so thick he could barely wrap his teeth around it. Most of it dragged across the rocks, and he tugged it toward Emi.

Emi's eyes widened. "Come, Max. Come."

Max inched the stick closer to Emi. With a final yank, he brought it to her trembling hands.

"Good boy, Max! Good boy," said Emi. She grasped one end of the stick between both her hands. Angling it down into the space between her stuck foot and the rock, she carefully guided a third of the stick into the inky hole. Bracing herself against the other end, she grunted and pushed with all the force she could.

The rock shifted a fraction of an inch. Emi took a breath and strained down on the branch again. She could see the limb bowing under the weight. "Don't break," she whispered through her teeth. She heaved down on the stick again.

"Grrrrrraaacccchhh!" she yelled as the rock trapping her foot lifted another two inches. She could feel the stick slipping in her hands. If she lost control, the rock could smash into her foot and she would still be trapped, but with a broken foot.

Max ran to the hole where her foot was trapped.

"No, Max!" screamed Emi. She squeezed her fingers as tightly as she could and readjusted her grip. Without breathing, she squeezed her eyes shut and heaved.

The rock lifted. Emi yanked her boot free from its stone prison.

Max stuck his nose toward the boot, sniffing.

"Max, move!" Emi cried. Her arms trembled as she strained to keep the rock from crashing down on his head.

As Max pulled back, Emi lost control of the stick. The rock whumped back down, missing Max's nose by inches.

Emi reached out and folded Max into her arms. In that moment, all she cared about was the dirty, smelly, trembling creature who had come for her. He had chased off coyotes and given her a way to free herself. He was still her Max, and he had found her and helped to set her free.

When she had run away from the house, she hadn't thought about how dangerous it would be for Max. She had been so focused on her own plan that she had been oblivious to the consequences of what could happen to him.

Max had gotten lost. He could have never found her and died in the woods, drowned or starved or attacked. The fact that he found her was a miracle, and she would not take that lightly.

She looked at Max. He had stopped breathing hard and looked back up at her with happy, tired eyes. "I've got you," she whispered as Max put his head down and made sleepy mumble sounds with his mouth. She would let him rest, and then she would bring him back to the cabin. They would be safe there for the night, until she could figure out what to do next.

She thought about her stay in the woods, and how she'd imagined it would be an act of triumph and defiance against the unfairness of life. She would survive on her own and teach the world that it couldn't stomp her spirit into the dirt.

But it hadn't gone that way. She had ended up cold and wet, full of fear and loss.

But she was also noticing every little breath Max took. The way his body rested against hers, full of trust and contentment. It was that, too.

Emi kissed the top of Max's sleeping head. And even though she was tired and hungry and scraped up and bruised, she didn't want to be any other way.

CHAPTER 24
MAX

Max's Guide to Being a More Responsible Dog

1. Have a lovely little nap and dream about catching squirrels.

2. Wake up in the arms of the girl. Snuggle close, then reach your head up and way backward to lick the bottom of the girl's chin. The awful loss you felt when you weren't with her is gone. You have the girl. And the girl has you.

3. Also, the girl has treats. Which she feeds to you. Hooray!

4. As you gobble them down, you realize it's been a very

long time since you've eaten. The treats feel like they fall through a hole in your stomach, because when the girl has given you all the snacks she's going to give you, you are still hungrier than you've ever felt before.

5. Follow the girl out of the boulder field and back into the woods.

6. As you trot beside her, out of the corner of your eye you see something.

7. SQUIRREL!

8. Feel a big glob of saliva fall from your lips. Every muscle in your body wants to leap up and give chase.

9. Don't.

10. Instead, step a little closer to the girl. Maybe too close because she almost just tripped on you. Oops.

11. Decide that from now on, if you do hunt, you will not run off. YOU WILL STAY WITH THE GIRL.

12. Or, at least, stay within eyesight of her.

When the girl stopped for a break under a tree, Max decided to do a perimeter search for anything edible. He rooted through the leaf litter, digging for spiders and bugs, but they skittered out of the way before he could lap them up.

Then he saw a slug that didn't appear to be moving too fast. He bit into it.

Ugh!

Max spit out the slug and slapped his tongue against his mouth, trying to get rid of the taste. Behind him, he could hear the girl quietly giggling.

He put his nose to the ground, sniffing and listening, senses alert, for anything that could be snack-like.

Below the ground, he heard a rustle and a scurry.

Promising? he wondered.

He followed the tiny pitter-patter carefully, nosing through a large pile of old leaf litter. The sound got closer and closer. He could almost feel the warmth of whatever tasty animal lay beneath the ground. He spotted a faint raised tunnel of dirt. It was a burrow.

Great—burrow hunting! He could do that and still stay

with the girl. Max poked his nose inside the entrance and inhaled in short, sharp bursts. There was something inside. He could smell it. He leaped onto the burrow and began to dig. Rotten leaves and dirt flew underneath him as he pawed the ground, rooting out whatever animal lived beneath.

Suddenly, a vole exploded out of the burrow.

Wow! I was right! There was *something there!* Max felt very proud of himself.

Out of the corner of his eye, he saw the vole hurrying away.

"Come back, snack!" he woofed.

The vole squeaked, then darted forward, narrowly evading Max's mouth as he bent down to grab it. He chased the vole at full speed as it hurtled across the leaf litter, around six pine trees, through a prickle bush, back around two of the trees it had just circled, then made a desperate plunge toward a dugout hole at the base of an old oak.

Max skidded to a halt in front of the massive tree. He was too big for the entrance that the vole had disappeared through.

He was just debating whether to start digging around the

hole to open it up when there was a high-pitched squeal and then silence.

A fox trotted out of the hole. Its mouth was red. Behind it, three tiny kits poked their noses out behind their mother.

Max drew back. The mother fox snarled and sprang, a lithe, wild creature protecting her cubs. Her teeth sank into his foreleg, and she yanked. Max felt the sting of his skin breaking, and a bolt of pain shot through him.

"Ow!" he cried.

"Max!" the girl screamed. Max saw her grab a stick. She tried to thrust it between him and the fox, but the fox held on to him with bitter determination.

"Stop biting him!" The girl wrenched off her backpack and hurled it at the mother fox. The fox unlatched her jaw from Max and leaped out of the way.

The backpack hit Max in his bitten leg full force. He staggered, whimpering as he scuttled away from the fox's den.

The mother fox slid in front of the den's entrance, her teeth bared, snarling.

Max tried to put some weight on his injured leg. The pain of it nearly blinded him. He lifted it up and hopped farther back, hoping the fox wouldn't dive in for round two.

She didn't. Gathering her kits, she hurried them back into her den, baring her fangs one last time at him before disappearing from sight.

"Oh no. Oh, Max, oh no," the girl said. She dropped to her knees as Max hobbled over to her and collapsed at her feet.

CHAPTER 25
EMI

EMI GATHERED MAX up in her arms and carried him to the river. As she bathed his leg with running water, waves of guilt crashed over her.

She never meant for Max to be in danger. When they had been reunited, she had thought that they would be fine. That maybe somehow they would be frozen in that moment of happiness forever. But time had continued to tick on, and now here she was, cradling her beloved, injured dog, who she had failed to protect.

Her hand went to her wrist, but there was nothing there. Inside her pocket, two broken pieces of jade pressed against her leg, reminding her that whatever belief she had in being protected was gone.

She shook her head. Right now, she couldn't think of her broken talisman. Max needed help, and he didn't have a lucky bracelet to keep him safe. He only had her.

She worked her fingers gently over his wound, washing away the dirt and the fox saliva that had embedded itself in it. When she was done, she lifted the limb out of the water. Blood flowed down Max's soaked fur.

Emi opened her backpack and found her long-sleeved shirt. She grasped the shirt between her hands and pulled. The stitches at the shoulder stretched and snapped apart.

She twisted up the torn-off sleeve and wrapped it around Max's leg. She tied the ends together to form a knot. When she was done, she picked Max up and carried him to a spot next to the river.

Max lay limp next to her, panting. She could feel his ribs rising and falling shallowly, drawn tight against his skin.

Emi sat, her hand resting on Max. He had followed her. He had saved her. She leaned over and buried her face next to his. She didn't care that he was dirty and stinky. She could feel her heart crumple into a misshapen ball.

Max whined softly and turned his head to gaze at her. His eyes were wide and dazed, but there was more than just pain behind them.

Emi knew that look. He was hungry. That was the reason why he had chased that vole into the fox den. Getting injured hadn't changed the fact that he needed to eat. And soon.

She sat up and dumped the rest of her pack out onto the ground to take stock. There had to be something that she could use to feed Max. Something. Anything.

She had a knife. An extra shirt, a pair of socks, underwear, and her hat in her stuff sack. A plastic water bottle, empty. The matches from the cabin. Her headlamp. And one small Ziploc bag half-full of gorp. After picking out all the chocolate pieces, she dumped the remaining peanuts and raisins in front of Max. He stuck out his tongue and slowly ate them up. When he was done, his head slumped back down onto the ground.

Max was in no condition to move. Her plan of going back to the cabin that night would have to wait.

Emi reached for her stuff sack. She pulled out all of her clothes and heaped them onto a pile over Max to keep him as warm as possible. Then she went to the river to think.

Right now, Max needed more food. *She* needed more food, too. She stared at the rippling water and tried to remember if anything in the Maine woods was edible. Roots and berries and nuts? Maybe, but all the berry bushes she had seen in the past few days were bare—they would not yield raspberries or blueberries for some time. And she had no idea what roots to look for, or even what a peanut or almond tree looked like.

She shook her head. She didn't even know if peanuts grew on trees.

In front of her, the water flowed by, curling around the riverbank in tight, white, foamy eddies. Rainbow-winged dragonflies and lanky-legged water skimmers glided across the surface.

Emi felt a sharp nip and looked down. A mosquito was stuck to her arm. She swatted at it and missed. She watched the mosquito fly out over the river, blood-swollen, making its getaway.

A red-bellied brook trout soared out of the water, its mouth gaping wide. A moment later, it splashed down and disappeared into the river, taking the mosquito with it.

Fish. Emi had been thinking so hard about what to eat in the woods, she had forgotten about the river and what it could provide.

First things first. She had no fishing rod, so she would need to improvise. After looking over her belongings again, she pieced together a plan. She got out her knife and cut a few small slits into the bottom and sides of the stuff sack. She opened the other end wide.

She took an empty water bottle and stabbed a few holes into it with her knife. Then she took it and went to the edge of the river. She began to dig into the embankment with her hands. Before long, she found what she was looking for—a wriggling pink worm. She fed the worm through the narrow opening of the water bottle. She continued to dig until she had eight long worms inside the bottle.

She got the stuff sack and placed the bottle of worms inside it. Then she found a short, sturdy stick. She took off her socks and boots, and waded shin-high into the river. She found a shallow spot with a pebbled bottom, hunting around until she found two rocks that were about the same distance apart as the width of her stuff sack.

She placed the stuff sack full of worms into the river and weighed down the bottom of it with pebbles. Then she jammed the stick into the mouth of the stuff sack to keep it open.

The stick stuck out at a diagonal. It was too long. Emi drew up the stuff sack and went back to the shore. She found another stick. This time, when she wedged it between the two rocks, it held.

Praying her fish trap wouldn't come loose, Emi took a breath and stepped away. The stuff sack held in place, undulating gently as water filled it.

Emi backed up and waited. A minute went by, then another, then ten. Her feet were getting cold, but she did not move. Her eyes were fixed on the stuff sack.

Suddenly, the sack flipped up and broke loose. Emi plunged her hand into the water. Her hands latched on to the stick keeping the sack open. It pulled free of the sack. She grabbed again, and her fingers found a nylon cord. She pulled, and the mouth of the stuff sack closed. When she held it up, water drained through the gashes in the sack as it danced in front of her.

She brought the sack to shore and unloosed the nylon string. She turned the sack upside down. A glimmering fish wriggled out and began to flop along the ground.

Emi swallowed hard. She picked up a rock. "Thank you," she said. "Thank you for feeding me and my dog, and for existing so we can be here tomorrow." She brought it down hard on the fish's head, and it stopped moving.

An hour later, she had four more fish lying in a row next to her belongings. The sun was sinking through the branches, and with it the warmth of daylight. As darkness fell, she gathered leaves and small dead branches, then piled rocks into a circle to make a small fire ring.

She arranged the wood—small pieces first, in a tiny,

fragile pyramid. She took the book of matches out of the bag and lit one. It flickered and died immediately. She took a second match and struck it against the matchbook. This time, she brought a hand to the match as soon as she lit it, shielding the delicate flame from the wind. She gently brought it down to her kindling. The flame leaped onto the wood and began to burn.

Piece by piece, Emi fed her fire until she had it crackling, with the smoke keeping the eager mosquitoes at bay. Then she went over to Max and picked him up. She carried him to the fire and laid him down next to it. He whined and lay still. His eyes were closed.

Emi took out her knife and picked up a fish. She cut off its head and made a long, clumsy slice through its belly. Swallowing hard, she scooped out the guts of the fish and flung them into the river. Then she skewered the fish on a branch and held it over the fire until the skin had blackened and was about to fall off.

She waited a few minutes for it to cool, then started to slip chunks of meat off the bones. When she was done, she had a pile of cooked trout that she brought over to Max.

Max started sniffing. Emi picked up a piece of trout and gently placed it next to Max's nose. He opened his mouth, and she fed the fish to him. Bit by bit, he ate the trout until it was gone. He licked Emi's fingers. Emi smiled. She got to work on the second fish.

By the time the stars had emerged in the sky, Max and Emi both had had their first real dinner in two days.

After Emi had thrown the bones into the fire and drank from the river, she curled up next to Max and held him as she watched the fire flickering against the dark.

She did not sleep. She fed the fire over and over again, making sure to keep Max warm.

As she sat, holding Max while the bright yellow flames danced before her, Emi thought about her foster parents, memories running through her like silk.

She thought about the first match she ever lit. Jim had given one to her the morning the fire had been too weak to last the night and had shown her how to coax the small, hot, teardrop-shaped flame from the tip of the matchhead into a crackling, bone-warming heat. He had trusted her with the small flame, both delicate and dangerous. It had been such a different feeling from what she had been used to—having everything taken care of for her because no one thought she could take on the responsibility of taking care of herself.

But now, out here in the woods, she had to be there for

herself—and for Max, too. Emi brushed her hand along Max's belly, his sparse fur tickling her fingertips, until it reached a small, round bump.

She frowned. Her finger went over the bump again, trying to figure out what it was. She tried to turn Max on his back so she could see his belly in the firelight, but a quiet groan from him made her stop. She reached over and dug her headlamp out from her backpack. She switched it on and shined it on Max.

His belly was crawling with ticks. Flat, seedy insects with spindly legs that pressed into her dog and mouths that were drinking his blood.

Emi felt like puking. She tried to ignore the disgust flooding through her body. Clamping her teeth down on her bottom lip, she reached out and pinched the body of the fattest tick she saw. It wriggled against her fingers, and she fought the urge to let go. Slowly, she pulled the tick from Max's skin until it let go with a soft pop.

She tried to throw the tick, but it clung to her thumb like barbed wire. She found a twig and used the end of it to scrape the tick off. Then she threw the twig in the fire.

As she watched the twig burn, Emi felt her heart thumping with rage and satisfaction. How dare that tick touch her

Max. How dare it. She went back to Max, methodically peeling the ticks off him. As she fed their bodies to the fire, their deaths filled her with fierce happiness. Pluck, scrape, burn, pluck, scrape, burn. It felt like she was performing a ritual, ridding her dog of the parasites that infested his body.

As Emi pulled off the last tick, Max looked up at her and whined. His tail thumped once, sadly.

Emi stopped, her eyes clearing as if breaking free from a spell. "Sorry, Max," she said. "I didn't mean to do that so hard."

This time, when she threw the tick in the fire, it was without venom. She sat back down and drew Max close to her. "Maybe this is how you felt when you were defending me from the coyotes," she said. "Maybe anger feels good and right when you're protecting someone you love."

She reached into her pocket and took out the two half circles of jade. In the firelight, they cast small shadows in her hand. Her voice caught. "My mom could be like that, you know. There was this boy in the neighborhood we lived in, Billy Hayward. He was the kind of kid that liked to give other kids atomic wedgies and kill ants by setting them on fire with a magnifying glass. One day, he pushed me into a snowbank in front of my house because I wouldn't give him my lunch money. Then he pinned me down and began to pelt my face with snowballs.

"My mom ran out so fast. I've never seen her so angry before. She pulled Billy off of me and tucked him under her arm like a football and carried him back to his house. She told me to wait outside while she went inside and had it out with Billy's parents. She never told me what she said, but Billy never bothered me again.

"After that, she gave me this bracelet for protection for when she wasn't around. And she told me that if it broke, I would have to throw it away and get a new one."

Emi brought the two pieces of jade together and pressed. "But I'm not going to. I'm going to put it back together and keep it. I don't care if it's not perfect. My mom gave this to me, and she is part of me. And even if the only thing of hers I have left is broken, it's still filled with her love."

She ran a thumb over one of the cracks. It was invisible, but she could still feel it. "You know, maybe perfect isn't the point," she continued. "When my mom gave me this bracelet, she wasn't telling me that I'd be safe forever. Just that she was looking out for me."

Emi looked at the bracelet one last time, then gently put the pieces back in her pocket. She patted Max on the head.

"Kind of like the same way I'm looking out for you, buddy. I can't be there for you all the time, but I'm always thinking of you, and I will do anything and everything to keep you safe."

Max laid his chin on Emi's leg and gently started snoring. Emi smiled and tucked her chin into her chest. She would snooze, but not all night. She had a fire and a dog to keep alive.

As she lay there, holding Max, she thought about what to do next. She was done thinking only of herself. Her dog needed shelter. He needed food and warmth and safety and a place where he could rest. Hopefully, tomorrow he could walk, and then they could go to the cabin and she could care for him there.

Is that really what he needs? a little voice inside her whispered. *Don't you think he deserves a little more than that? Like a real home? Like, perhaps, adults who would know how to properly treat an injured dog?*

She thought about how Jim and Meili would know how to treat Max, even if his injury was worse than a sprain. They were knowledgeable. And patient. And kind. Not just to Max—to her, too.

Maybe she had misjudged what they would do when the

baby came. Maybe what they were trying to tell her before she had run away was that they would figure something out. That the news would be good—for all of them. In the months that Emi had lived with them, not once had they shown her anything other than support.

But fueled by her fear of betrayal, she had betrayed them. She had fled to the woods thinking they would tell her she wasn't wanted, like all the times before.

There was a part of her that ached to open herself up to her foster parents. To admit that she was scared of not belonging anywhere, and to have them comfort her and tell her that more than anything, they wanted her to belong with them—her *and* Max.

A wave of sadness engulfed her. No. To do that would be to make herself too vulnerable. She wasn't going to get her hopes up, only to be abandoned again. She would build her iron castle with iron walls around her, and only Max would be allowed inside.

"Max just needs me," she whispered into the empty night.

But as Max snuffled and whimpered in his sleep, Emi wasn't so sure.

CHAPTER 26
MAX

WHEN MAX WOKE the next morning, the girl was looking at him with tired, worried eyes. He lifted his head, and she stroked behind his ears softly.

His tongue stuck to the roof of his mouth. Thirst clung to the inside of his cheeks. He felt like he had just swallowed a bowlful of cotton balls. He staggered to his feet and hobbled to the river, dipping his tongue into the flowing stream. The water was cold and clear. It helped to push away the fog that was creeping across his brain.

When he was done drinking, he limped back to the girl and laid down.

The girl lifted up his leg. Max closed his eyes. He clamped his teeth together, but he could not stop a whine of pain from escaping his throat. The girl gently peeled back the rag around his wound. Fresh blood trickled through.

The girl took out a bag and unzipped it. She removed a small tube and uncapped it. She applied a layer of clear gel to the bite and then wrapped his wound back up.

When she was done, she went to the river. Max watched as she lowered a little black bag into the water, like she had done the night before. She stood in the river, waiting, her hands poised over the fish trap.

The girl waited. And while she did, Max curled up in the morning sun. He tried to forget the hunger in his belly and the ache in his leg, but the pain kept him awake even though he wanted desperately to nap.

He heard a shout. The girl was splashing through the water. The bag had come loose and was drifting down the river.

Max lunged to his feet, ready to chase the floating sack, but a ribbon of pain threaded through his leg. He sat back down and watched as the girl plunged after the fast-moving bag. Only when it finally caught the current and picked up speed did she admit defeat and wade ashore, soaked up to the waist, to rejoin him.

She changed out of her clothes and squeezed the water from her pants and socks. She laid them out in the morning sun. Then she reached into her pack and pulled out her food. Max wagged his tail. He could smell the delicate odor of peanuts and sugar.

The girl looked at him for a long time. Then she picked up a bar and peeled off the wrapper. Instead of chomping down on it, he watched as she began to scrape the sides of the bar with her front teeth, raking away the brown outer layer of the bar. When it was almost gone, she put the bar in her mouth to dissolve the last bits of the layer. Then she took it out of her mouth and laid it in front of Max.

Max sniffed the wet bar. Then he picked it up with his teeth and crunched down. A sharp, giddy happiness over-whelmed him. Never had a bite of food tasted so good. He swallowed, and half the bar went down his gullet. One gulp later, he had devoured the bar entirely.

The girl took out two more bars. She scraped off the brown layers and fed the rest to Max. When he was done, his leg was still spiking with pain, but he felt well enough to stand up and hop on three legs.

The girl got dressed again, packed her belongings, and took one last look around. Then she called to Max. When he came to her, she patted his head. She checked the water. Then she turned and began to walk upriver.

Max cocked his head. A spike of hope filled his heart. He

couldn't be sure, but he thought that there was something familiar about the way they were going.

Maybe they were going back home!

A joyful yip spilled out of his mouth, and his tail sprang up. Max walked as fast as he could to the girl and began to lick her hand over and over. It was the only time he wasn't searching for crumbs.

They followed the river around a bend. Max trotted by the girl, still limping but with a kick to his gait. He had seen the trees before, had sniffed the wet pebbles at the water's edge. He knew where they were and where they were going.

But as he rounded the bend, he caught the faint scent of something familiar. He stopped and looked away from the river. The scent was coming from the woods, away from the girl and from the way home.

Max bent his head uncertainly. He sniffed in short, sharp breaths, trying to focus on the one scent out of millions that were flooding his nostrils. He closed his eyes and willed all the other scents to disappear.

And then the scent came to him again. He straightened. He knew what it was and who it belonged to.

It was Red. His friend. She was out there, she had survived the bear, and she was probably looking for him. He had to get to her to tell her that he was okay and that he had found the girl.

Ignoring the stabbing pain in his leg, Max ran to the girl and began to bark as loudly as he could. She looked down in surprise. She pointed toward the river.

Max grabbed on to her pants cuff and tugged. He bared his teeth and growled.

"No, Max! We're not going that way." The girl pulled her cuff from Max's teeth. She pointed to the river again. "We're going *this* way," she said, and began to walk in a firm, straight line alongside it.

Max tried to latch on to the girl's cuff again, but she brushed him off. All of a sudden, he felt the fatigue of his muscles set in. He knew the smart, right thing to do would be to follow the girl.

But it wasn't about loyalty to her right now. It was about helping his friend Red find him so they could all go home together. Max turned and plunged into the woods. The girl cried out. "Max!" she yelled. "Max, no!"

Max froze for a second out of obedience. But then he pushed on. He hobbled into a thicket, wincing as burrs dug into his skin and clung to his fur. He heard the girl yelp as the burrs found her, too.

The girl's hand grabbed at him. Max leaped forward. Her hand closed upon his tail, but he strained forward, and his tail slipped through.

He limped as fast as he could away from the girl. Then he ducked his head and sniffed. Red's scent was stronger. Much stronger. He could almost taste it in the air now.

Max ran through the woods, with the girl behind him, chasing him. He did not let her out of his sight. But even though his leg ached, he did not allow himself to be caught.

Just as he came to a clearing and Red's scent became overwhelming, Max caught a whiff of something else.

Something was near. Something big.

"Gotcha!" The girl had finally caught up with Max and made a flying leap to tackle him. Even as she closed in on him, her arms avoided his injured leg.

"Why are you misbehaving now?" she asked him.

Max barked and wiggled frantically against her arms. He had to show the girl where to find Red! He had smelled her there, right in the field ahead of him. He struggled free, a whine in his throat.

The girl's eyes widened. Her limbs froze against Max, rigid. She had seen something.

Max stopped in his tracks and looked, too. There, next

to a half-rotten tree at the opposite edge of the wood, was a giant bear.

It stood, putting its paws on a tree trunk and arching its back. Above it, Max saw a cream-colored hive buzzing with bees.

The bear latched on to the bark and began to climb, shuffling its body upward. When it came to the hive, it reached out toward the hive and tugged. A honeycomb, swarming with angry insects, plummeted to the ground.

The bear shambled down and picked up the honeycomb between its paws. It bit into the comb, devouring the honey, wax, and bees, until the comb had all but disappeared.

The girl pulled Max behind a tree and held him, trembling. They listened as they heard the bear making its way toward them. But then, suddenly, the sounds stopped. A deep growl filled the air, and they heard the bear turn and move away, picking up speed as it went.

Max strained his neck around the tree and looked to where the bear was heading. When he did, his tongue, normally so slobbery, went dry.

There, in the middle of the clearing, hunched over a ball of bloody fur and paying no attention to what was around her, was Red.

CHAPTER 27
RED

RED WENT BACK to the river. There would be fish in it, and although she hated getting wet, food was food. She was just about to wade in when she spotted a flash of movement.

Gopher.

Red's stomach growled. She sprang at it—plump, a juicy morsel—paws outstretched.

The gopher squeaked and darted away, slipping through the grass with desperate ease.

Red chased it away from the river and through the forest. It was a fast gopher, and it wasn't until she came to the middle of a wide, bright clearing that she finally pounced and made her kill.

After not having eaten in days, her whole world became the feast at her paws. She bit and swallowed and bit again, gulping her meal in large, raw chunks. She was in heaven—so much so that she forgot to remember where she was until she heard the ragged ripping of brush and branches.

Red looked up from her meal. Out from the edge of the field, a bear came galloping toward her, swallowing up the ground in frighteningly long strides. Red could smell the rough power of the animal, the musk of its shaggy body. She could see the stark hunger in its yellowed eyes. Its skin hung loose from its skeletal frame like an oversize coat.

The fur on Red's back flew straight on end. She hissed and spat, her tail puffing out as she faced the creature.

The bear peered down at Red, shaking its head side to side as if it couldn't believe that it was being challenged by something so small. As if it expected Red to roll over and become its easy meal.

Red leaped up and swatted at the bear. Her claws sank into its soft, sensitive wet nose. Quick as lightning, she unhooked her paw and jumped back.

The bear's eyes darkened with fury. It bore down on Red, raising its paw to retaliate.

Red ran. She abandoned the gopher carcass and fled to the edge of the wood and into the brush, twisting easily through the smaller openings that the bear had to wrestle through. Even so, it gained on her.

Red spotted a small, beetle-eaten opening in the side of a fallen log. With a desperate instinct, she forced herself inside. She huddled, hearing the bear draw near, knowing that if it wanted to, it could tear through the decaying bark as easily as it slashed through the honeycomb.

Claws thumped into the log just above her. Red waited, ready with her teeth and nails to confront the bear when it came ripping through the soft wood.

But just as splinters of rotten log fell onto her head, a scream pierced the woods. It was the girl's voice. High, angry, and powerful, it carried with it a call of pure defiance.

The girl was coming for the bear. To challenge it. To tell it that she was in charge.

She's going to get herself killed, Red thought as the claws slid off the hollow log and the loud, lumbering scuffles of the bear moved away from her.

But, to her astonishment, against all her practical judgment, she thought something else.

But then again, maybe not.

CHAPTER 28
MAX

Max's Guide to Learning How to "Sit"

1. Feel the girl tap your nose and whisper, "Sit. " She brings her face up to yours.

2. You whine and take a step.

3. The girl says that same pesky word again.

4. Pause. Try really, really hard to understand.

5. The girl kisses you, and then stands up and starts moving toward the field. Toward the bear and Red.

6. Run toward the girl, barking and woofing.

7. Get side-tackled by the girl, but gently. Even though she catches you, she makes sure not to touch your injured leg.

8. One more time, the girl says, "Sit." She is looking at you as if whatever she has just said is the most important thing you will hear.

9. Suddenly, visions of bone-shaped treats flood your eyes. Something clicks deep inside your brain, and you finally know what the girl is asking you to do.

10. Sit.

11. Hear a muffled cry of joy and accept the girl's embrace. Although you are suffocating just a little bit from her crushing hug, see that it means a lot to her that you know this word.

12. "Sit," the girl repeats. "Stay. I'll be back. I promise."

Max sat and watched as his girl left the edge of the forest and began to head toward Red.

He watched Red fly through the field, the bear following her, and the girl following the bear. If Max hadn't been so worried for them, he would have thought that it was an excellent game of chase. One that he would have never won with his hurting leg.

Red reached the other edge of the field and darted into the side of a fallen log. The bear whuffed and chuffed as it dug into the log with its claws, leaving raw slashes through the bark.

Max felt his hackles rise. Instinctively he knew that if he drew the bear's attention away from Red and to himself, there was a good chance he would not survive. He was injured and all hobbly and could not outpace an animal of that size.

But at least he could try to distract the bear. He opened his mouth to bark. But before he could, he heard the girl yell.

She yelled and waved and beat her hands together.

The bear turned. Its claws stopped raking the log.

The girl picked up a stick and began jabbing it in the air toward the bear. Then, to Max's astonishment, she put her head down and ran full tilt at it.

The bear snuffled and huffed and swayed uncertainly. Then, when the girl continued toward it, yelling, "Back! Back!

Move! Go! Shoo! BLLLAAARRGHHHH!" it stumbled back, confused, then turned and careened off into the woods, rustling through the bushes as it went.

"And STAY away!" the girl cried.

Max felt an upswelling of love for the girl. His girl had chased away the bear. His girl had been brave and protected Red and helped save her when he couldn't.

Max knew then that he would never leave the girl. That she was his, and he was hers.

CHAPTER 29
EMI

EMI HAD NO idea how the cat knew Max, but when it came out of the hollow log and rubbed its fiery red head against his leg, she realized that it had a connection to her dog that she would not question.

And when the cat came up to her and rubbed its head against her own leg while Max woofed and barked and pranced about her on his three good legs with that goofy smile on his face, Emi knew she had done the right thing by scaring off the bear.

She had astonished herself. Thinking on it now that the danger had passed, she couldn't believe what she had done. She had confronted one of the biggest beasts in the woods, and she had prevailed. Probably by raw luck, but still. She had not turned away.

As she began to head back to the river, with Max glued by

her side, the cat came, too. Emi realized that she had become leader of a little crew of three. She had to think for them all.

It seemed like the safest thing to do would be to go back to the hunting cabin. After gathering up her backpack, she began to retrace her steps up the river.

The river straightened into a wide, rippling line for half a mile, then flattened out even further as it began to twist and bend again. Every once in a while, Emi would catch sight of a tree that bent in a particular way that seemed familiar. She didn't know if they were retracing their steps exactly, or if the small flashes of recognition of the woods were something her mind was making up to reassure her, but she trusted the river.

Her trust was affirmed when they rounded a bend in the river in the early evening, and the cabin where Emi had spent two nights before came into view. Her heart jumped, a shout of triumph on her lips. They were halfway home, and tonight, they would not be out in the darkness in the woods. And tomorrow, maybe tomorrow, they would be home.

She fished that evening using a rod and reel she found stowed behind the cabin and brought in three trout, which she cleaned and cooked over a fire and fed to Max and the cat, picking out the bones, until they were both satisfied. Only after did she quiet the rumblings in her stomach, eating the last crispy fish and sucking her fingers clean as she watched the fire dancing against the stones of the fire ring she had created.

She had never been so hungry, and food had never tasted so good. Right now, if she were given the choice of a fire-blackened trout or a Pop-Tart, she would have chosen the fish. It nourished her in a way that reminded her of Meili's cooking—hearty and real, made with effort instead of loaded with the sickly sugar that often made her mood crash an hour later. As the stars filled the darkened sky, Emi felt full and happy and sure.

As night deepened, Emi sat and listened and watched the river and felt an unsettling peace come over her. Nothing was perfect, but there was a stillness in her heart she hadn't felt before. Here, in the woods, next to her dog and her cat, she felt as though thick, warm, invisible, and unbreakable threads were connecting them all to one another, and to their surroundings. She leaned over and buried her face in their fur.

As the fire died down, she gathered the animals and shuffled them into the cabin and onto the bed with her, Max by her feet and the cat by her head.

As Emi felt tiredness wash over her, she thought about what she would do next. When she first left, she thought she had a plan, but it really hadn't been one. Now she had had to make decisions not only for her to survive but also for Max, and this cat as well. She had to be responsible.

And that meant going back to civilization. As fearful as she was of what it meant to step back from the woods, she knew it was the right decision. Just as she had faced the bear, she had to face her fears of abandonment and rejection and find a way to move past them instead of hiding from them.

She was tired and dirty and aching, but as she fell asleep to Max's snores and the cat's purring, she felt as though it was exactly where she was meant to be.

The next morning, Emi woke to the sounds of the river and birdsong. She went to the water's edge, Max by her side, and splashed her face, rubbing the insides of her eyes to wake up. She was wiping off her face when next to her she saw a flash of red. She knelt down.

There were wild strawberries growing by the riverbank.

It seemed as though Maine had edible berries in June, after all. Emi plucked one and popped it in her mouth. Sweetness flooded her tongue, better than any candy bar. She ate another, and then another. Beside her, Max did the same.

When their mouths were stained pink with berry juice and their bellies were full of breakfast, Emi and Max returned to the cabin. Emi packed her things and got ready to leave.

"Kitty?" she called, then called again. And again.

The cat was nowhere in sight.

CHAPTER 30
RED

IN THE MORNING, Red had left Max and the girl to hunt down her own breakfast. A few hundred yards from the shack, she spotted tiny oblong tracks haphazardly zigzagging through sand on the riverbank. She went over to them and sniffed, taking in the faint scent of fur, the blurred outline that meant the tracks were older than she would have liked, calculating the size of the creature that would make that kind of impression.

It was a bunny. Good meat. She followed the tracks as they rushed crazily from one tree to another. The tracks grew fresher, until Red could see the sharp outline of the pawprint and the faint crumple of lines of the individual pawprints.

Breakfast was nearby. Her nose quivered as she entered a clearing. She could smell the bunny now, plump and delicious, and very close. Her belly howled.

There was a pile of something in the field. Red loped over to it. It was the bunny. Half of its body was missing.

Suddenly, everything came into focus. The zigzag of the bunny's tracks hadn't been haphazard—they were the line of an animal running from a predator.

In an instant, Red knew that something was coming back for the rest of the bunny. It was too much of a meal for a wild animal to give up.

Red's tail shot up. Her long fur puffed out, making her seem twice her size. Moving her head from side to side, she scanned the edge of the forest for hunters. She saw none.

Her stomach growled. With her eyes riveted to the tree line, Red bent down and took a bite of the rabbit. No coyote or fox appeared out of the woods to chase her. She took another bite.

The air shivered above her, and Red realized her mistake just as a pair of talons sunk into her shoulder. She twisted onto her back and lashed out with her claws as the hawk's beak sliced down onto the side of her cheek.

Red felt a flash of pain as a chunk of her fur came off. Howling and spitting, she wriggled out from under the hawk's talons. It opened its wings and gave a bloodcurdling cry.

Before the hawk could attack again, Red charged. She

leaped at the hawk's chest, slashing out and biting, trying to reach the vulnerable skin beneath all its feathers. The hawk tipped back its head and drove down, piercing Red's flank. It hopped onto Red and dug its talons into her fur. Pounding the air with its wings, the hawk began to pull her up.

Everything seemed to slow down. Red saw the ground fall away from her. She could hear the beating of wings and feel the rush of icy air against her wounds. She could feel herself slipping into inky black unconsciousness. She knew if she let the darkness take her, she would never wake up.

Reaching up with her good foreleg, Red swiped blindly. Her claws lodged into the hawk's leg. She bit the hawk's leg as hard as she could.

The hawk screeched and opened its talons. Red let go of it and fell back, feeling a gush of blood spill from her side as she plummeted. The oldest of her instincts kicked in, and she flipped upright, landing on her feet.

The hawk circled above her. Red could feel its rage and its hunger. She did not begrudge it. Like her, the hawk was a hunter and a fighter. And if it chose to attack her again, she wouldn't blame it. She was deeply injured—easy food.

The hawk folded its wings and dove. As it bore down on her, Red bared her teeth and raised a stained red paw, knowing she could do nothing against the onslaught. But even though she knew she couldn't win, she was still ready to defend herself to the last scratch.

The hawk's talons dropped. But instead of pouncing on her, it shifted its flight a fraction to the right of Red. She watched as it scooped up the remains of the bunny and lifted its prey effortlessly into the clear blue air.

Limping to the edge of the field, Red hid herself in the nook of a tree. She tried to lick her streaked fur, but her head fell into her chest. She was very tired. Curling herself into a small, tight ball, Red closed her eyes and waited for darkness to take her.

CHAPTER 31
MAX

"RED!" MAX BARKED. "Hellloooo? Where are you?" He tried to sound casual, but something felt wrong. He and the girl had been waiting for Red to come since morning.

The girl had packed her bag and looked ready to go hours before, but she hadn't beckoned for Max to follow her away from the cabin. Instead, she had sat near their fire ring with him and they had waited. And waited. And waited.

Now it was midafternoon, and Max was worried. Red would have told him if she was going out for long. Because that's what friends did. And she hadn't and so something must have happened to her.

"Max," the girl said when Max jumped up and sniffed around the cabin for the hundredth time, "we just have to be patient." She patted the ground next to her, inviting him to come and sit.

But Max was done with sitting. He wanted to know where his friend was! He went around the cabin in wider and wider circles, until he caught the scent of something.

It was furry and familiar and it was Red.

Max ran to the girl and barked at her three sharp, short times. Then he went back to where he had caught Red's scent, looked at the girl, and pointed his nose in the direction that Red had gone. He kept on swiveling his head, back and forth, girl, Red, girl, Red, girl, Red, until the girl got up and started coming over to him.

This time, it was Max who led the way. He followed Red's scent beyond the cabin, into the woods, sniffing with sharp, sure breaths. Finding her was his mission now, and that was all that mattered.

He came to the edge of a clearing. Suddenly, his nose caught the smell of blood and fear. He stopped short and looked out. His tail tucked into his legs, and his ears drew back. There was a mound of fur streaked with crimson in the middle of the field.

Max whined. He walked slowly over to the red stain. Nothing was there. He turned his head and saw drops of blood speckling the early summer grass on the far side of the field.

He found Red, barely breathing, at the foot of the tree. "Red," he called. "Red?"

Red did not respond.

Max nudged Red with his nose. The cat's mouth opened in a silent meow.

"Hang on, Red," said Max. He licked the cat's matted head. Then he began to run.

The girl had not been far behind him. Max woofed and grabbed a pant leg, tugging at her gently.

"What is it, Max?" the girl asked.

Max backed up, and she followed him to the edge of the clearing.

The girl gasped when she saw the huddled mound. She knelt down and gently folded Red into her arms.

CHAPTER 32
EMI

THE CAT WAS in bad shape. Emi cradled it to her chest, her touch feather-soft, half expecting to feel it struggle in the indignant sort of way that cats do when picked up, but it did nothing.

With the cat in her arms and Max by her side, Emi began to head back to Jim and Meili's. She did not run. She did not wander. Instead, she strode with deliberate, determined steps, energy flowing through her in sure, even pulses.

She had purpose. Her duty was to keep this broken, wild creature alive. Everything came into sharp focus—the veins of the leaves on the young maple and alder and birch trees, the chocolate-colored dirt beneath her feet, the wizened, twisted roots and unexpected rocks she stepped over instead of tripped upon—all of it.

As she flowed through the woods, Emi never felt more

powerful. She knew where she was going, and as she worked through the miles of woods and river behind her, she could feel herself pulling toward the two people in the world who she realized she could trust.

It felt so much better to be running toward something instead of away from it. Emi realized she was no longer afraid of what was going to happen to her when she had others to protect. She felt good. She felt strong. She was bound for home.

When she finally spotted the familiar house with its straight, shingled roof, her lungs opened and she drew a long, relieved breath. She had never been so happy to be back at a foster house. She hurried up the steps and pulled open the front door. Behind her, Max followed at her heels.

Jim and Meili were sitting at the kitchen table, hands clasped, Missing posters with Emi's face on it strewn everywhere. When they turned to see Emi, it was as if time had stopped, hovering on the moment of her in the doorway, clutching the dying cat, lit by the afternoon sun, returning to ask, finally, for their help.

"You're back!" Meili cried. "We've been scouring the woods for days. The whole town is searching for you!" She jumped out of her seat and rushed toward Emi. Behind her, Jim hustled to do the same.

"I'm so, so, so sorry," Emi said. "I shouldn't have run away from you, and from the baby, and what I was afraid you might tell me. I left because I thought I could make it on my own. But I can't. I need you. Both of you." She could feel tears slipping down her cheeks.

"Oh, love," Meili said. "We need you, too. You have brought joy and wonder to our little house, and we want you to stay. Forever."

"That's right, Emi," Jim said. "We wanted to tell you that we wanted you as much as we wanted the baby. And that you were going to get to be a big sister, if you would have us for a mom and dad."

Emi smiled as she felt her heart crack open. "I would like that," she said. "I would like that very much." A salty drop fell onto the bundle she was holding, and her eyes widened. She wanted more than anything to give Jim and Meili a hug, but there was something more important she had to do first. "Please, there's an injured cat, and I don't know how to help it," she said, and gently laid the cat on the table.

The cat lay limp on its side. The skin on its neck had been split open by two deep gashes. Its hind leg had an ugly wound that was still bleeding. Half of its face was crusted over with dried black blood.

"It's Red," said Meili softly. She knelt down and ran a careful hand over the animal's body. She turned to Emi. "This cat used to belong to the people who owned this house before us. When her owners moved, she was off hunting in the woods. They stayed for two days past their moving date hunting for her but finally couldn't wait any longer." She sighed. "The woods finally got you, poor girl."

"No," said Emi. She pointed to the cat's belly. It was moving slightly up and down. "She's still alive. We've got to save her."

"Emi, one thing you'll learn about living in the woods is that things die," Jim said. "Red has got a lot of injuries. I doubt she's going to make it."

"Please," said Emi. She hadn't come all this way just to have her parents tell her that there was nothing they could do. Her voice cracked as she said, "We have to try."

Meili stood up. Her mouth set in a thin, purposeful line. "Okay. But you have to promise me that if you try to keep her alive and she ends up dying, you won't blame yourself."

Emi nodded.

"All right." Meili went to a cupboard and got out an electric shaver. "She's got a lot of fur that we need to shave off if we don't want her wounds to get infected. I might need your help holding her down if she struggles."

But Red didn't move at the low electric whine when Meili plugged in the shaver and turned it on. She didn't flinch when Meili pressed the shaver to her skin, or when the woman cut off hunk after hunk of the glorious silken fur that kept her so warm. When Meili was done, Emi gritted her teeth at the sight. The cat lying motionless was half the size of the injured, magnificent wild creature she had gathered in her coat. She looked tiny. Helpless.

Below the table, Max whined softly. Emi knelt and gave him a fierce hug. "Red is gonna be all right, Max, " she said, even though she wasn't sure it was true.

"I'm getting my first-aid kit," Jim said. "Boil some water and get some rags from the drawers."

Emi ran to the kitchen. She took the teakettle off the counter and filled it. She tamped the cover onto the kettle and set it on the stove. When she pushed the burner knob and turned it, she heard the click of the pilot as it caught the burner. Flames danced under the teakettle. Emi turned the flames up as high as they would go.

When steam leaked out of the lip of the kettle and it began to wail, she took it off the stove. She poured the water into a bowl and took out soft, clean white dishrags from the drawer next to the stove. Then she returned to the cat.

Jim had laid out the first-aid kit next to Red. Meili took the bowl of hot water and the rag from Emi. She dipped the rag into the bowl and squeezed out the excess water. She began to rub Red's wounds. The rag turned a dull pink as she worked.

Once she had cleaned out Red's wounds, Jim applied lines of antibacterial gel to them. Then Meili rummaged through the first-aid kit and pulled out a thin, clear tube.

"This is skin glue. I'm going to close her up with this." Jim broke the seal of the glue and squeezed the gooey liquid onto the cat's neck gashes. Meili pinched the skin together.

Red began to twitch.

"Hold her still," Jim said.

Emi placed her hands on Red's limbs, just where the legs pulled into the body. The cat's fur seemed to shimmer under the glow of the kitchen lamp. "You'll be okay," she whispered over and over again, as if she were chanting a spell. "We're here. And you'll be okay."

As she lightly stroked the giant red cat, she glanced at Jim and Meili, who were cleaning up the bloody rags and matted fur.

"Thank you," said Emi. She swallowed hard. "I'm . . . I'm really glad you both knew what to do."

Meili smiled. "Us too," she said. She and Jim went up to Emi, and with Max by their feet, all of them settled in to keep watch.

As they gazed over the cat the color of glowing sunset, Emi moved closer until her head just touched Meili's and Jim's shoulders. They gently put their arms around Emi, and together they watched over Red late into the night.

CHAPTER 33
RED

FOR A LONG time, everything was dark. Then she heard sounds that bumped against her, soft and blurry like swimming fish. She did not understand them. Everything ached. She closed her eyes and slept.

When she woke, the girl's face was close to hers. There were circles under the girl's eyes. Her eyes blinked, and her face lifted into a hopeful smile.

Red closed her eyes and slept again. She slept while the ravaged, broken parts of her body knit themselves back together and the marrow in her bones slowly pumped out new blood that replaced the quart she had lost. She slept as her slashed face became a scarred face, full of tough tissue that bumped over the place where the hawk had torn open her skin. She slept until one day she woke and was able to stumble to her feet before collapsing.

She was not used to the ungracefulness of healing. She had been the strongest of her litter, the fastest sprinter, the best hunter. Now it was as if her body had changed into something she did not recognize—functional but clumsy, with disused muscles melting into small, shapeless bumps. She could not run. Even her walk was a strange half limp, half crawl as she dragged herself across the floor.

When she was able to recognize the floor, and the walls surrounding her, she realized she was in the house she had lived next to for so many years. One day she was able to jump to a window ledge to see the shed where she had spent her days after the boy with the freckles and hair the same copper as hers had left.

There was still no boy. Only the girl. And the dog who had found her.

The first sound Red remembered recognizing after the hawk attack was the thumping of Max's tail. She opened her eyes and glared at him.

"You're awake!" he barked.

"You're being extremely loud," Red muttered. "Take your tail and go somewhere else."

Max retreated to another room, but Red could still hear his tail whacking against the floor. Despite herself, her tiny smile stretched across her mouth before she sank back into unconsciousness.

It took her months to recover. The girl made her a bed from a little cardboard box lined with an old blanket and set it by the window so she could see the outside world. She watched as young summer days became longer and sleepier. She saw Max playing fetch and ball and running around in the front yard, collar on, leash off. She watched the woman's belly grow and the way Max, with all his energy, seemed to gentle down next to her. How the girl would press her head to the woman's stomach and giggle at the sounds she heard within. How the family gathered at the kitchen table, meal after meal, talking and laughing and learning from one another as their lives unfolded in the thick summer heat.

By the time Red was well enough to go outside, the air had turned crisp and the leaves, once so brilliantly green, were tinged with flecks of red and gold. She found a spot in the sun and breathed in the warm, fresh air. As the days grew even cooler, she still preferred the shed to the house. But when it rained and a new ache tugged at her neck and her shoulders, she was content to slip back into her family's house and curl into her box as the girl stroked her newly grown fur.

CHAPTER 34
MAX

Max's Guide to Being Happy

1. Wake up. Stretchyawnfart.

2. Lick the girl awake.

3. BREAKFAST!

4. Roam around the house while the girl goes to school. Sometimes with Red, sometimes on your own. Never go too far.

5. Be there waiting for the girl when she comes home. Thump tail, woof, feel that bursting feeling in your chest like you always do when you see her.

6. Accept head rubs, hugs, and all manner of pats. Only get slightly annoyed when the girl's bracelet, mended with glue and still very beautiful, bumps you on the nose.

7. Spend time with the girl and the rest of the family, including the bossy new baby who pulls your ears and makes a lot of sound when you lick its toes but seems to be very loved by all.

8. DINNER!

9. Curl up by the girl's feet.

10. Go to bed loving and being loved.

ABOUT THE AUTHOR

Meika Hashimoto is the author of *The Trail*. She grew up on a shiitake mushroom farm tucked within the rural mountains of Maine. After graduating from Swarthmore College, she worked in the mountains before taking a job as a children's book editor. She now lives one valley over from her childhood home with her husband and two rescue dogs.